THE GREEN SOLDIER

BY J. EDWARD GORE

ISBN-13: 978-1-7335252-2-0

In loving memory of Grandmother and Aunt Christine

With special thanks to
My wife
My parents
Zack
Bud and the 9th Ky Infantry

Written for my children, nieces and nephews

November 6, 1924
Hardyville, Kentucky

My dear Lenwood,

I never really knew my brother till after he died. Although my skin has long since wrinkled, it remains my greatest regret.

It was many years after the Great War and with considerable personal cost that I finally obtained all of these documents. Please forgive your great-granddaddy's writing. I was fourteen when the letters began and never dreamed I would one day teach school.

As I held you in my lap yesterday for the photograph, I knew I needed to write you this note. You're only a baby now and won't be reading the letters until you are a young man, but one day your father will give them to you. I have not altered anything, regardless of how painful it is for me to read some of it now. For better or worse, this is your heritage.

May the Lord bless you and keep you.
Your loving Great-Granddaddy Jim

| _G_ | 13 | **Ky.** |

John J C Gore

Pvt, Capt. Towle's Co., 13 Reg't Ky. Inf.*

Age _19_ years.

Appears on

Company Muster-in Roll

of the organization named above. Roll dated

Camp Cobson Ky, Dec 30, 186_1_.

Muster-in to date _Dec 30,_ 186_1_.

Joined for duty and enrolled:

When _Sept 18_, 186_1_.

Where _Camp Andy Johnson Green 5th Cor Co._

Period _3_ years.

Remarks: ....

....

....

....

....

* This organization subsequently became Co. A, 13 Reg't Ky. Inf.

Book mark: ....

Chandler

Copyist.

CHAPTER ONE

January 12th, 1862
Campbellsville, Kentucky

Dear Jimmy,

I finally had a spare minute to sit and write a spell. When I first showed up in Campbellsville where the regiment was getting together, there was a man in uniform at a small table holding a pencil and thumbing through a stack of papers. I said goodbye to Papa and got in line. Of course I was nervous, standing in line and hearing the same question being asked over and over again. I wasn't listening to the answers. It all sounded the same. The longer I waited, the more I could feel my chest move with every heartbeat. It was cold, but my scalp was starting to itch like when it's too hot.

Finally it was my turn. The man didn't look up but said in a bored voice, "Next. Name?" I paused as I was trying to speak. He still wasn't looking up but asked again, a little irritated, "Name?" I started to speak but knew it was going to be a bad day. I'd been struggling some even with talking with Papa that morning.

Finally I did get out "John G-G-G-G-G-Gore." He put down his pencil and looked up but didn't say anything. He didn't smile, but didn't frown. He repeated my name and I nodded yes. He then directed me where to stand with the others. I could feel men around me staring and could hear whispers that were likely about me. I looked around to see if I could spot Joshua but I didn't see him. I later heard he joined a different regiment to be with his cousin. I wish he would've been there.

Next we were mustered into service of the United States Army. We raised our right hand and repeated a pledge that Colonel Hobson read out loud. Thankfully nobody around me seemed to pay any attention to my attempt at repeating it, so I just moved my lips without any sound. After saying those words, or at least what I could, I became the property of the Federal army. I do what they tell me to do, whenever they tell me to do it. And that's fine with me. I didn't feel like I was running my life anyway. You know how it is on the farm.

But here I have a chance to prove myself. Everyone thinks I'm stupid because of my stutter. They think because I talk slowly that I think slowly. Well, when you have a medal on your chest, you don't have to talk. When other men salute you because of a higher rank, that's respect. I don't know how I'm going to get promoted or earn a medal, but I'll figure it out. I believe that's why I'm here. It's what I'm supposed to do.

The colonel fought in the Mexican-American War and got a medal. I heard when he was fighting he didn't even notice his arm had been shot. From what I've seen, I believe it. A couple of days ago the sergeant told me to give the colonel a message. The colonel was looking straight ahead and I went up beside him and said "Sir," but he just kept staring. I got nervous and then my tongue started getting stuck. I tried to say it again but I sounded like a snake. It was a bad *S* day. Then I felt like he was ignoring me on purpose. I didn't know what to do but could feel sweat on my brow. Finally I tapped him on the shoulder. He sort of woke up and said he was sorry. I was just glad he didn't get mad.

The message from the sergeant was that we were finished drilling and were going to practice shooting. I hadn't talked with him before and he didn't know I stuttered. He looked me in the eye, which as you know always makes it worse. Now I was really nervous and was trying to say the whole message at once, but couldn't get anything out. It's such an awful feeling to know what I want to say but the harder I think about it, the worse it gets. After struggling for what seemed like forever, he put his hand on my shoulder and said, "It's okay son, just take your time." I took a deep breath and then was finally able to get it out. He asked my name and with some stumbling I was able to tell him. He turned away from me and looked off into the woods, but asked me to tell him more about myself. So I told him about Ma and Papa, Thomas, Lucy, and even you. I talked about our crops and critters for I don't know how long. I don't remember how I got to talking about it, but somehow I started telling him about milking Susie. He turned around, raised his eyebrows, thought for a bit, and thanked me for delivering the message. A week later we were drilling, that is practicing our marching, and he told the sergeant we were as graceful as a three-legged cow. He looked over at me and gave a wink.

I wish I could write that everyone was understanding of my stuttering and treated me nice. Right after we got mustered Colonel Hobson introduced our captain and then our drill sergeant, a man named Hickman. He was the same man who had checked me in. He's as tall as me but stouter. The colonel told us to do as he says, no matter what. When Sergeant Hickman first talked to us, his voice was soft and easy. I was glad he wasn't one of those loud sergeants I'd heard about. But just because he doesn't yell doesn't mean he's nice. I don't think a dog would go to him if he had bacon in his pocket. He says he believes in justice. One soldier, Isaac, overslept morning roll call last week and had to hold a brick in each hand with his arms stretched out all morning. I've seen the sergeant get his hackles up and I was sure he was going to shoot Isaac dead a couple of times. But he didn't. The sergeant called Isaac everything but a talking mule, but he never raised his voice. It ain't right how he can be so mad but sound so calm.

I made a mistake one day when he asked me a question and I answered, "Yes sir!" He let me know quickly that he wasn't an officer and ordered me to say "Yes, Sergeant!" It was too much. I was helpless. My tongue was like a donkey that's locked his knees. Hickman's eyes narrowed and he ordered me to say the words or else he was going to hang me by my thumbs. But I couldn't. He might as well have asked me to jump to the moon. I tried to speak. God help me I tried, but it just wouldn't come out. Thank God the colonel came by at that moment and saw what was happening. He called the sergeant over. I couldn't hear what the colonel said as the sergeant stood at attention. When the sergeant came back over he ignored me and we were dismissed. He mostly ignores me now, treating me like a cripple. The worst is that he talks slowly to me. I hate when people do that.

I like Campbellsville although it's been wet. We had ten days of rain to start the year off. There's a tavern called the Golden Horse where I get sarsaparilla. I like to just sit in there and listen to men talk. There was a fat man in there the other day that smelled like onions who said the war was about freeing the slaves. Other men jumped to their feet and argued with him and it almost came to blows. It's the silliest thing I'd ever heard. The colonel brought his slaves with his family to our camp. Do you think he'd fight to free his own slaves? I don't know of one soldier in our regiment who'd fight against slavery. I know I wouldn't. Before the colonel I didn't even know anyone who owned slaves. They don't bother me and I don't bother them.

I'll write again real soon.

Take care,
Johnny

January 18, 1862

Johnny,

Thanks for the letter. I ain't gonna lie. I've been waiting for it. We're all the same here. Ms. Johnson's cows got out again and I helped round them up. I was afraid that ornery bull of hers might get me. You know the one with one horn going up and the other going down? He's as mean as the devil. Papa says if you hold a cow's tail down to its back it won't kick. Well, maybe that's true, but I don't know how you could ever get close enough to that bull to find out. Besides, that won't keep him from giving you the horn. And that bull knows how. Ms. Johnson was so happy to have them back she gave me a chess pie she'd just baked. I'd planned on taking it home but I could tell it was warm and it was a long walk. First I was just going to take a bite but by the time I got home all I had was an empty tin and some crumbs. I sneaked around back to wash it out but just as I was starting to pump the water Ma walked up. "Son, what do you have there?" I turned around and must've looked like I'd seen the Holy Ghost. She started laughing and went inside. Later when Papa came in for supper she said I'd been given a pie, but somehow it went missing. He didn't even look at me, but just said, "That's mighty generous, Jimmy. Mighty generous."

Charlie came over the other day and we climbed up the cedar trees and then jumped down. Course I had a couple of times when I hit a hole in the branches and fell a little too hard on a limb, but we didn't break any bones so it was okay. Now Ma and Papa don't like me falling in the trees. Ma's afraid I'll get hurt and she'll have to mend me. Papa's afraid I won't be able to work. But when you fall down a large tree all the way to the ground it's a lot of fun.

It's exciting to get your letters. I want to hear all about your camp and soldiering. Please write and tell me something about what you're learning.

Jimmy

January 26th, 1862

Dear Jimmy,

Ms. Johnson does have a mean bull. She needs to hitch him to a donkey. It's one of the funniest sights I've ever seen. Mr. Seward had a bull that needed to be broke and so he tied a chain from the bull to a donkey. The bull would try to drag, but the donkey locked his legs and wouldn't budge. The bull tugged and tugged but the donkey never moved an inch. Once the bull tried to stick the donkey with a horn and the donkey turned around and kicked him in the nose. He didn't try that again. After a while the bull just sat down and then went wherever the donkey wanted. I remember watching it with Papa and asked him, "When will the bull get to drink?" He turned and said, "When the donkey's thirsty."

I met a couple of boys, Abraham and Andy, who I really like. Most all of us have nicknames now. One of the older soldiers saw Abraham eat another boy's leftovers and said, "My goodness son, you'd eat the scraps a hog would throw away." Since then, Abraham's been known as Scrap. He's pudgy with dark wavy hair and has lazy eyes. Only when something's important does he pull his eyelids all the way up. And sometimes, his voice cracks. Once when the sergeant asked us which regiment we were in, Scrap squealed "Thirteen!" in a little girl's voice. He quickly cleared his throat and then gave a deep "Thirteen." We all shook, trying to hold in the laughter till we were dismissed. Even the sergeant gave a rare smile.

Andy's called Pole. Scrap said if the rebels attacked, Andy could always hide behind his rifle with room to spare. Pole's hair looks like a handful of red straw and his skin's as white as a frog's belly. His family has ten kids with seven boys and three girls. He's one of the younger ones. He and his brothers wrestle all the time, making Pole tough in a fight. I've seen bigger men go a round with him only to end up yelling "Calf Rope" in a couple of minutes. Unlike Scrap, who's always having a big time, Pole's quiet. Scrap and Pole are my closest friends, my pards.

I've been given a nickname, too. One day when we were just standing around, the sergeant was in front of our tent, talking with a captain. Scrap was inside the tent and thought it was just Pole and I standing outside so he exited bottom first and made a loud explosion. We weren't at attention so we fell down laughing. I swallowed my tobacco. As soon as it happened my stomach started turning, cause I knew what was coming. Sure enough, I was in the sick tent for two days, asking myself why I chewed in the first place. Scrap came by that first day and said I was "green as the river." So Green's been my name ever since. The officers and sergeant call me "Private Gore." Nobody calls me John.

I wish I could get more books around camp to read. There's a few short novels that are passed around but they're not worth the hour it takes to read them. They tell the same boring story of a boy that loses his girl and then gets her back. I've seen a few other boys keeping a diary. But I think instead of writing one, which could get lost or stolen, I'll let my letters to you be my diary. This way it's already delivered and safe. You just have to make sure and keep them together and don't lose them. I'd appreciate you doing this for me. I've always worked hard at writing since I stutter. Now I have something worth writing about.

Take care,
Johnny

February 8, 1862

Johnny,

You still didn't tell much about soldiering. Either you're going to tell me a little or I ain't gonna write.

Did you hear about the secesh blowing up Green River Bridge? Just in case you hadn't, Simon Buckner ordered to blow it up before our troops got there. To pour salt on it, he had Mr. Key set the charges. But it didn't all blow up, just one of the trestles. Our troops are already fixing it. One of the charges didn't fire at all and some of the men around here got it out. Now that's a job I don't want. Can you imagine? Course I'm half-surprised that Papa didn't hire me out for two dollars to get it. But don't give him any ideas. Now I wonder if Mr. Key didn't really want to blow up the bridge in the first place, seeing how he built it. Ma said she heard Mr. Key had been worrying himself sick over having to blow up his bridge, spending a week in bed and not wanting to eat. Course I wouldn't know about the eating part. I ain't ever worried that much.

There's been a lot of sick men at the Federal camp around Munfordville. They've moved from a low place at the edge of a cemetery to a high place just outside of town. I don't know why they'd pitch a camp next to a cemetery anyhow. That can't be anything but bad luck. They might as well find a litter of black cats and paint a red X on their tents. Papa said Dr. Bentley came around and mended them and most got better, but a couple died.

I've heard Ma chewing the fat with Aunt Mattie the other night. They were going on and on about you joining up. Aunt Mattie got all teary eyed and said, "When they're little they step on your toes, when they're older they step on your heart." Ma got quiet for a spell, then she started talking about quilting. I don't know what they're worried about, you're the best at getting through the woods as anybody I know. And you're the best shot I've ever seen. Oh we'll all be glad when you're back, but not before you get some of those medals!

Do you remember Bobby Keebler? Me and George had been out hunting all day. I got four grey squirrels. They're a lot better than the old tough fox squirrels. Anyway, we walked by George's house and dropped him off and then I was headed back home carrying the squirrels. I was almost home, could even see the big Oak. And then Bobby stepped out.

"So where are you going with my dinner?"

"Your dinner? You mean you're so sorry you can't kill your own game? What are you, a buzzard?" His face started turning red and I could tell what he was thinking so I just said,

"Yep, you heard right. Now let me by."

Well, he knocked me down. He is bigger than me by twenty pounds at least and he took my squirrels. There was snow on the ground and he shoved some in my face and in my mouth. I was so surprised I didn't say anything. He knew he scared me cause he got a lot braver. He stood over me with his boot pressing on my chest, saying,

"Don't ever let me hear you sass me again. You hear?"

Him and his beak-like nose. I always thought he looked like a hawk. But he took my squirrels and I had to explain to Papa that I missed all my shots. Bobby's going to get his. Just you wait.

Jimmy

February 12th, 1862
Campbellsville, Kentucky

Dear Jimmy,

If I could come home I would. I'd march to the Keeler house and get ahold of Bobby. Let's just say he wouldn't mess with you again. I read your letter and was so mad I started packing my tent and told Pole I was going home. Thankfully he talked some sense into me before I made a mistake that would give the sergeant an excuse to hang me up by my thumbs. I let him read the last part of your letter because I didn't want the extra frustration of not being able to get the words out. He told me there would be plenty of time to pay the little weasel back.

Marching has been a lot tougher than I'd thought. When we first started, the sergeant was about ready to give poor Albert a bad beating. He asked him, "Don't you know your left from your right?" Turned out Albert didn't. Then the sergeant asked how many others didn't know their left from their right and a dozen raised their hands. He then had a corporal tie straw to one foot and hay to the other. So they marched around hearing, "Strawfoot! Hayfoot! Strawfoot! Hayfoot!" for hours until they got it. And if one of our company messes up, we all have to stay out in the field and practice until he gets it right. Now nobody wants to make a mistake. We're getting better.

You've asked me to tell you about soldiering and fighting so I'll tell you about how we fire in a line. During a battle we stand in two rows called ranks. A pair, a man in the front and the man behind him in the second row, makes one file. I'll draw it out for you. Now I'm just drawing six soldiers but in a company there's supposed to be a hundred.

X = firing gun   O = not firing gun

```
OOO                    No Fire
OOO

X X x                  Fire by Company
X X x

XXX    OOO             Fire by Rank
OOO    XXX

OOX    OXO   XOO       Fire by File
OOX    OXO   XOO
```

File by file goes down the line, and as soon as two men fire then the next two fire. After you fire you reload and wait till it's your turn. This way somebody is always shooting. Our officers like this when they want to keep the rebels from charging. Fire-by-rank or fire-by-company will send a strong volley, so you can knock out a bunch of their men all at once. Of course, the less of them standing, the less guns firing, which is good for us.

Make sure and remind Ma to send an extra blanket. I don't care if it's one they put over a horse, I just want to stay warm. She can also send some jars of food. I'm not too particular, anything sounds good now. We've marched enough to be in Virginia, but we haven't left Campbellsville. I've heard that we're going to head south soon. I can't wait.

Oh, and I met a girl.

Take care,
    Johnny

| _C_ | 13 | Ky. |

John J. C. Gore

Pvt., Co. A, 13 Reg't Kentucky Infantry.

Appears on

Company Muster Roll

for _Jan. & Febr._, 186 2

Present or absent _Present_

Stoppage, $ 100 for

Due Gov't, $ 100 for

Remarks:

FROM SECOND AUDITOR'S ROLL.

Book mark:

Chandler

(858)   Copyist.

CHAPTER TWO

February 18, 1862

Johnny,

A what? A girl? Lord Johnny, don't you have enough to worry about without a cotton-picking girl? She'll take your mind off of fighting, mark my words. And you know the rebels won't care if you have a girl or not. You need to set her aside and keep your mind on what you're there for.

I liked learning about how you stand in line and fire. I wish I could sneak down to Munfordville and hang around their camp. I know Papa'd skin me alive and Ma would do worse, but I got a bad itch all over to wear a uniform. I love the idea of doing something instead of farm work. Anything. I'm tired of critters and crops. I'm almost fifteen so it won't be long now.

Over the last few weeks Bobby ain't said anything to me and I ain't said anything to him. Oh, he said, "Those squirrels was some good eatin Jimmy." But he was just trying to get a rise out of me. I'm not paying him any attention for now. Don't worry, I haven't forgot. I'm going to get him sometime soon.

Jimmy

February 24th, 1862
Bowling Green, Kentucky

Dear Jimmy,

Well since you asked about the girl, I'm happy to tell you. Several weeks ago while we were still in Campbellsville I was sent into town to fetch a few packages for the colonel. When I got there I saw that the boxes were too big to be carried under each arm. I thought about carrying them stacked on top of each other, but then I wouldn't be able to see where I was walking and I was afraid I'd drop them and break something important.

As I was standing there thinking I heard a voice behind me ask, "How are you going to pack them?"

I was just looking at the boxes and said, "I don't know. I guess I'll just have to stack them and walk sideways so that I can see where I'm going. I just don't want to trip over my own feet." I wasn't paying any attention to anybody so I wasn't stuttering.

The voice answered again, "Or you could ask somebody to carry one while you carry the other."

I still hadn't looked behind me and then asked, "Yeah, but who am I gonna get to—"

I never finished my question because I turned around and saw this girl. But she wasn't just any girl. She's about as tall as you but with brown hair under her bonnet. I wish I knew how to describe her eyes better, other than to say they were big and dark brown. I could've stood there and looked into her eyes all day and it wouldn't have been long enough. She smiled and I tripped backwards over one of the boxes. I never felt

19

so clumsy or weak. All I could say was, "Hey." She laughed a little and said she'd be right back. I just stood there and nodded my head up and down for half a minute. I finally woke up as she returned with her little sister. She carried a box while I carried the other and we talked the whole way. Well, she talked and I smiled. I'd nod my head every so often. I don't even remember how heavy my box was. It could've been a hundred pounds or ten, I wasn't paying it any mind. Her sister walked on the other side of me, looking up at me as if I were a general. The little girl didn't say much, but when I'd look down at her every once in awhile she'd giggle and turn red. She was a cute little girl with light hair and blue eyes.

When we reached camp, after walking for a good half hour, my new friend told me if I wanted to write her a letter she'd write me back. I didn't have any paper on me so I just wrote her name on my hand, although there's no way I would've forgotten it. Her name is Annie Elzey. She smiled as she said goodbye and then as I turned around there was Scrap and Pole. Both of them were grinning ear to ear but I didn't mind. I could barely even hear what they were saying. I'm going to write her. And I know you're not going to understand what I'm going on about, but when she smiled it made me feel like I'd swallowed lightning. There ain't a girl around Hardyville that can hold a candle to her. She's seventeen, so a couple of years younger than me. I know it doesn't make any sense to you now, but just wait. One of these days you'll take a fancy to a little girl yourself. And when you do, you'll be glad your ol' Johnny knows what girls like to hear. Don't worry, I'll be happy to teach you.

It was just a couple of days before meeting Annie that Sergeant Hickman gave us our gear. You'd have thought he was handing out gold. We've been eating, sleeping, and marching like soldiers, but still wearing our same old farm clothes. Now we look like soldiers. Our pants are gray wool, scratchy but warm. The coat is blue and thick. Women from a few surrounding counties made them. I traded around for a couple of days before finding ones that fit. The boots were stacked in a heap so we spent almost an hour trying them on. Scrap said he could tell a left shoe from a right, saying these were some of those, "crooked shoes," but for me it was like sexing a frog.

We've been marching south and I've heard that we're going into Tennessee, but I don't know where. I hear a lot of rumors, but nobody really knows. At least nobody that will tell me.

By the way, send me some tobacco. I hardly ever chew since I swallowed it, but I can fetch a good deal for it here.

Take care,
Johnny

March 1st, 1862
Nashville, TN

Dear Ms. Elzey,

I don't know if you remember me or not. I'm the soldier you helped carry a package to my camp a while ago. I really enjoyed talking with you and appreciated your help. Your dress was very blue.

I hope you're not too cold with the late snow. It's been really cold here. Say hello to your little sister. She smiles a lot.

I'm with the 13th Kentucky Infantry, A Company, so if you have some spare paper then perhaps you'll find a minute or two to write me a letter. My regiment has marched down to Tennessee and we're looking to do some fighting soon.

Take care,
John   Gore
Private U.S. Army

March 15, 1862

Johnny,

Everybody here's all excited over the battles of Forts Henry and Donelson. Too bad you couldn't have been there and helped General Grant beat the rebels. They're calling him "Unconditional Surrender" Grant on account of his initials and when he gave the details for surrender he said "Only an unconditional surrender will be accepted." I heard Mr. Seward say General Grant likes to smoke cigars so now folks are sending him boxes of them. I'd send him a box myself if I had the money. I asked Papa if we could send him a couple of cigars. He just looked at me. I wish Grant would come through Munfordville. He's one general I'd like to see.

The way I heard tell, Grant just ran right over the rebels at Fort Henry and all the secesh hid in Fort Donelson like a bunch of rats. Then the rebel generals inside their fort thought they were too important to get captured, so they snuck out on the river during the night. All except for Nathan Bedford Forrest, he rode out with his cavalry. At least he wasn't a coward. Later a newspaperman asked Grant about the rebel generals sneaking away and he said, "If I'd caught them I'd turn them loose. They do us more good by leading their troops than sitting in our prison."

I told you I was going to get Bobby back and I did. We had a warm Sunday last week before it got cold so we decided to have a spring church picnic. Bobby and Albert went down to the creek below the church and I spied the can he used to drink. Well, I poked a little hole in the bottom of it. When it was time to eat and we were all sitting down I went and got water in a pitcher to pour for everyone. I poured his glass first, cause I knew he was thirsty. I was pouring everyone else and then I heard all kinds of people laughing and carrying on around where he was. I went over and acted surprised. Sure enough, he had water all down his shirt and pants. It looked like he wetted himself. Everyone was laughing at him. It was the best. He showed out, turning red and yelling at Albert. What a great day.

So are you going to be fighting soon? Since Grant just won at the Kentucky-Tennessee border and you're so close, you might get your chance. Make sure and write plenty of letters if you get in a battle to let me know what it's like. Reading about Grant makes me want to join up today. I know, I know. I promised I'd wait till you got back. It's just exciting, that's all.

Jimmy

March 17th, 1862

Dear Pvt John Gore,

Well of course I remember you! Do you think I carry packages for you lazy soldiers every day? I'd need to get my own uniform. Winnie says to tell you hello. She'd never seen a soldier up close before so she didn't say much while we were walking, but once we dropped you off she didn't shut her mouth for three days. I was afraid she'd forget to eat.

It has been cold here, but we ain't had any more snow. March in Kentucky seems so sad and gray. It makes me look forward to the colors of spring that much more.

I figured that if you can't manage to carry two boxes by yourself then you likely don't have a warm blanket to keep you from catching cold in the winter, so I've started knitting you a blanket. Nothing too fancy mind you, but you're not going to be any good to the army if you're sick with cold.

I didn't think about it at the time, but you didn't tell me much about yourself. At least tell me where you're from and something else about you.

You look after yourself,
Annie Elzey

March 29th, 1862
Dickson, Tennessee

Dear Jimmy,

How's home? You'll be happy to know it's starting to get interesting around here. You wouldn't believe how far we've marched—over two hundred miles since leaving Campbellsville! It's okay. I'm not complaining. It doesn't do any good anyhow. Still, my feet have blisters healed over with tough hide. I bet a snapping turtle couldn't bite through the calluses. I'm told we're somewhere between Nashville and Memphis, headed west.

It looks like I'm gonna get my turn on the field. I'm ready to quit training and start fighting. Everybody here says he's itching to get in the war. If you listen to Scrap you'd think he'd already taken out a hundred rebels himself. I just hope it's an actual battle and not just a march. Sometimes when one general sees he has no hope of winning he surrenders before there's ever a gunshot. That's fine for them but doesn't help me. I need this.

We've had sad news recently. A couple more boys from my company have died from loose bowels, what we call the "Quick Step." I'd never thought about soldiers dying outside of fighting. It's hard. At the funeral they put a cloth over the drums to make the beat softer. It's a sad sound. The colonel wrote letters to the boys' families. I heard he wrote a different letter for each soldier. I expect that's what the questions about home were for.

Thanks for the tobacco but send more hidden in newspapers and socks. There's one officer that goes through our packages for it. We haven't found out who he is yet, but we will. Give Tom and Lucy my love and of course Ma and Papa.

Annie wrote me a letter a couple of weeks ago. I was scared she may not want anything to do with me, but she was nice in her letter. Her little sister's name is Winnie. She's a cute little girl and her Pa will have to keep a loaded gun when she gets older to keep the boys away. And don't you worry yourself about Annie. I know what I'm doing. All day long we march, march, march. Thinking about her keeps my feet and arms from hurting so much. The gun gets awful heavy after packing it all day, especially when the sergeant forgets to let us change positions. Some weeks I don't get to leave camp and we can't get visitors inside, so it gets lonely. She said she's knitting me a blanket for winter if the war is still going on. I don't care if it's not fit to put on ol' Red, I'll look after it like it was stitched out of gold, because she knitted it for me and she was thinking of me while she was making it. I'm going to write her another letter. I don't stutter when I write.

Mind yourself with Bobby. He may not be high on brains but he's stout for his age and has a mean streak. You're even now so I'd leave him alone.

Take care,
Johnny

April 6th, 1862
Savannah, Tennessee

Dear Jimmy,

I know I just wrote a letter last week, but this is it. Yesterday the colonel talked about getting to "see the elephant," which means to fight. We've been marching nonstop for a few days to help Grant. He's in trouble. The rebels surprised him and did a lot of damage so now some are calling him "Unprepared" instead of "Unconditional."

Tonight we arrived at Savannah and took a ferry up to Pittsburgh Landing. We floated down the river in large flatboats with a couple of men using long poles to guide us. We were standing around talking about what it was going to be like getting in a battle. Then Scrap and I saw some logs bobbing up and down in the river. We couldn't really see them until the moonlight gave us a clear view. They weren't logs. They were bodies. Nobody said anything after that, just an occasional cough. It smelled like when we butcher a couple of hogs, except there weren't any hogs. For the first time in my life I was glad I was hungry. If my stomach had been full it would've turned.

We landed on the shore and couldn't believe what we saw. Men and boys were crawling around on the banks like worms. We heard, "Order rest for fifteen minutes." Now usually when we hear that order we let out a loud "Ahhhh" to let the officers know we're tired. Nobody did tonight because we were too distracted. Scrap, Pole, and I saw a soldier lying down with a red scarf wrapped around his leg. He was old, probably around forty. He looked like he'd been run over by a team of mules. Pole and I stared at him like he was made out of cheese, but Scrap spoke up, "What was it like?" The wounded soldier mouthed "Water," and Pole gave him a couple of swigs. He warned us to fill our canteens cause, "Everybody's thirsty in Hell." Then he looked towards the river and said, "God, it was awful. Those gray demons screamed and never stopped." I didn't know what to say. We filled his canteen and propped his head up. Then we heard the order to get back into line.

Just after that it started raining and we're wet to the skin. I just hope my caps and cartridges stay dry. I'll admit that after seeing those men at the riverbank we were all pretty low. The colonel saw the looks on our faces and decided we needed a speech. I don't remember all of it, but here were a couple of good lines.

"The day is here to stand, to fight, to win. They'll shoot, they'll charge, they'll yell, but meet their end."

His speech wasn't long, but it hit the spot. It was the kindling needed to help restart a fire inside of us. We're resting now and there's been a break in the showers, giving me a few minutes to write. I hope I'll be writing again in a few days.

Take care,
Johnny

April 9th, 1862
Pittsburgh Landing, TN

Dear Jimmy,

I'm glad you're reading this letter and not another. That's about as good as I can say for the last few days. There's so much to tell. I feel like the last week has been a month.

The night of April 6th we stood in formation, along with the Kentucky 9th, the 19th Ohio, and the 59th Ohio in a field just to the rear of the 41st Ohio camp. Colonel Crittendon was in charge, but Colonel Hobson was close by. We waited all night in the rain, hoping for dawn. I never missed the sun so. Couldn't eat or relieve ourselves. Just stood there getting wet. After eight in the morning we saw it. A thick fog turned into a gray and brown army. I couldn't make out faces, but I could hear their sergeants barking. Our bugle ordered advance. My legs felt like I was pulling a wagon. They fired and so we formed our lines and fired back. We shot and shot and shot. I tried to pick out a target instead of just firing into the line, like Papa said if you're shooting at a flock. After going at it for what only seemed like a few minutes, the barrel was so hot I could hardly touch it, as if I'd been firing for an hour. I looked over at Scrap and he was counting out the steps to load his gun as fast as he could, which wa a good idea. There were crashes, curses, and screams as I'd never heard before.

When the shooting stopped I looked at Scrap and Pole. Both of their eyes were wide open, and I expect mine were too. At first I felt really good that I had been in my first fight and did my duty like I was supposed to. I was proud of my company too. We all did good. But then I looked on the field and saw men lying on the ground. Some were moving a lot, some a little, some not at all. Men on our side of the field, men on theirs. I was getting low on caps and cartridges, like most of the other men, and we were ordered to fill our pouches up for another round of fighting. I didn't have time to sit around and talk with Scrap and Pole about our first fight. I wish I had.

At about nine o'clock in the morning they pulled back and we advanced several hundred yards to the Hamburg road. It was important we control that road to cut off their retreat. We marched through the woods for an hour and a half till we met them again. This time they attacked and were as mad as a wet hen. While Colonel Hobson was giving orders his horse was shot from under him. We were advancing and there were dead rebels on the ground that we were walking over. Scrap was several steps ahead of us and then turned around to say something. Behind him I saw a rebel that had been lying on the ground make it to his feet. The rebel was bloody but picking up his rifle with a bayonet on it. He was going to stab Scrap. I could hear Scrap's words but I wasn't listening. I was trying to warn him but my tongue was stuck. I tried. God knows I tried. Just as the rebel was raising his rifle Scrap stopped speaking as he looked at my eyes. The blade went through his chest and both of them fell down. I don't know where everyone else was looking but as Scrap fell Pole and a couple of other boys ran over and made sure that rebel wouldn't ever rise again.

I ran over to Scrap, pulled the gun out of his back and turned him over. I tried to tell him I was sorry. I finally got out a "Sorry" after several tries. My tears fell and cleaned out a path down his face black from gunpowder. He pointed to his breast pocket and moved his lips, but I couldn't understand what he said. He choked and gurgled. Then he was gone. His eyes stared straight ahead without any light. Those eyes knew me just a second before. Now he was a large, lifeless, bloody doll.

Folks have laughed and stared at me cause I couldn't talk most of my life. I knew my talking would be with me forever like a rock in my boot, but I never thought it would cost me a friend's life. I don't know why nobody else was looking at him. I don't know why he'd been walking ahead and then decided to turn around and talk. I don't know why I couldn't speak. All I needed was two words, "Look out!" or "Behind you!" I've said those words over and over to myself now and I can say them fine. But I couldn't say it when it counted. I'll never forget those last few seconds, watching him die, wanting to go back to yesterday more than ever before in my life.

When Granddaddy died he was old and you were very small. On his last morning I still remember seeing this big, stout man so weak he couldn't mash together his butter and molasses. Papa had to do it for him. He hadn't ever said anything to me when I went off to school before, but that morning he did. "Goodbye, Johnny. Be a good boy." He put his heavy hand on my head and smiled. Papa came to school a few hours later. We walked all the way home before he knelt down, put his rough hands on my shoulders and told me. Course now I know Granddaddy was sick, but I didn't know it at the time. He never complained. We were all sad, but he'd lived a full life.

But Scrap's death wasn't like that at all. At nineteen he was just ready to start living you might say. He wasn't just a number on a casualty list to me. He was my pard. I'd read about men dying in battle, heard about it, even seen it in our first fight, but there's nothing to describe when your friend falls and you could've helped. I looked into his eyes as the knife went through his chest. Just before that moment he knew I was trying to warn him. But I failed. I didn't know what to say as he was on the ground dying, I did know what to do once he died. I took the letter from his breast pocket and cut off a small lock of hair to send back to his parents. He would've done the same for me.

I looked up as I took out his letter and another boy from our regiment, John Jacobs is his name, was staring at me. He didn't say anything or make any gestures with his face but I felt that he knew what I'd done. Or what I didn't do.

Then I heard the yell. That high-pitched sound that makes the hair on your neck stand up. I was shaking, but my hands moved faster than I thought they would. My fear turned to anger. I wasn't fighting for country, Lincoln, or the 13th. Somebody was going to pay for Scrap.

I saw a rebel coming my way, and since he chose me I was going to let him have it. As he closed in, I could make out a dirty, skinny face. Just before we met, everything got quiet. I could tell by how he was holding his gun he didn't know what he was doing. I pushed his blade aside and then plunged mine into his chest. It went all the way in and I could feel the crunch. He looked into my eyes and started gasping. His face changed to that of a boy's about my age, surprised and scared.

He didn't die right away. I pulled my blade out and he fell down. He coughed up blood and wiggled around for a while. It wasn't how I thought it would be. I looked at my blade with the red stain on it. I've helped slaughter livestock for years, but this was different. This was human blood.

"Lookout Green!" I turned and another rebel was charging. This man was older than me, storming like a mad bull. But he stopped short to see how I would move. He was smarter than the first one. He wasn't afraid. We made several jabs at each other until I tripped and fell. He smiled. I remember thinking this was it. This was how I was going to die. I heard a shot and the rebel fell back. Pole came running up, "That was close! C'mon lets go!" I couldn't move. Scrap was dead. I just killed a man. And Pole just saved my life. Pole could tell what I was thinking and said, "Well what'd you think I was gonna do, let 'em kill you and then shoot?"

We pulled back several hundred yards. Colonel Hobson came around, preaching one more sermon about the Hamburg road. Again, he got us fired up to go out and fight. After getting some more bullets, powder, and caps, we got to it. We charged for the next couple of hours and shoved the rebels back. I shot at several and think I nicked a few, but I'm not sure.

It's different when it's far away. But even with all our fighting, they were able to retreat. Once they got away, we didn't chase them. The rain was beating down so hard it hurt your skin and there was no taking shelter. That was yesterday. It's clear today.

Last night before going to sleep, Pole and I sat and talked about Scrap for I don't know how long. We remembered all his funny pranks and silly sayings. We told story after story and both of us laughed until we could hardly speak. Course it was after hours so we had to whisper. When we finished telling everything we could think of we were quiet for several minutes, like sitting around after a big meal. We said good night and I told him I needed to go out and relieve myself. I got away from everyone and cried. I didn't make much noise, but I cried till I couldn't cry anymore. I couldn't help it. Ever since I was little Papa would tell me to act like a man and not cry. Papa's never lost a friend like this. I couldn't tell Pole that when Scrap needed me most I failed and it might happen to him. I want to fight for my country, but if I cost another life like this I'll have to leave.

I told myself that I would be honest in your letters, as these will tell my story of being a soldier. I didn't want to write all of this, but I felt I had to. I needed to do it to honor Scrap. Besides, after writing it I can breathe deeply again.

You won't be reading any new stories about Scrap. And that's what I miss the most.

I'll write when I can.

Take care,
    Johnny

April 18, 1862

Johnny,

We were all sitting easy after Junior's folks came over and showed us his letter that said you were alive. Papa just knew you'd been shot and were lying in a ditch somewhere. He's having a harder time with your soldiering than Ma. He goes into town every chance he gets to keep up with the news. He'll read the same paper over and over, as if the ink is going to change. I'm glad for planting season just to take his mind off the war. Course we've already set out potatoes, and we've planted cabbage, peas, and radishes.

I know you said I should leave Bobby alone, but the other day at school he tripped me right in front of everyone else and I broke Mary Hamilton's water jar. I didn't mean to but I couldn't help it. I got a paddling and had to tell Papa when I got home. He always said if I got a whipping at school he'd give me double at home. Well, he made good on his word.

Just when we was even Bobby had to go and do this. Don't worry, I'll get him. You mess with the bull and you're going to get the horn.

Sorry about your friend. But you can't blame yourself for Scrap getting killed. You didn't kill him. That rebel did. You were brave in getting that other rebel and at least you didn't get yourself killed.

We've heard of some of the folks around here getting treated rough by Federal soldiers, not rebels. I'll let you know if I get any particulars.

Jimmy

| G | 13 | Ky. |

John J. C. Gore

Pvt., Co. A, 13 Reg't Kentucky Infantry.

Appears on

Company Muster Roll

for Mch. & April , 186 2

Present or absent Present

Stoppage, $ 100 for

Due Gov't, $ 100 for

Remarks:

Book mark:

Chandler

(858)   Copyist.

CHAPTER THREE

May 5th, 1862

Dear Jimmy,

I got your last letter, but it seems like it takes forever for them to get here. I haven't heard of any Union soldiers stealing or attacking regular folk. You may have just heard rumors that the rebels started. I wouldn't worry about our boys.

You need to leave Bobby alone. Now I know that Papa always said not to back down from anyone, but I don't think you're going to like where this ends up.

Here at Pittsburgh Landing we won the battle because they left first, but nobody's bragging. What I realize now is that by winning, we get to enjoy the spoils of war. And by spoils, I mean the wounded and the dead. After the enemy retreated, we checked on the wounded. We looked after our boys first, then theirs. We quickly figured out that all those who died would have to be buried and we weren't too happy about it, particularly digging graves for the secesh. None of us signed up to be grave diggers. I was cold, hungry, and mad. Mad to be in such an awful, miserable place, having to do a chore worse than I'd ever imagined.

And then I came across a young rebel that looked about your age. He was sitting against a tree by himself, crying. His tears streaked white on his gun powdered cheeks. He looked up at me and asked, "Why don't you just go home and leave us alone? Why are you coming down to steal our farms and take away our families?" I wouldn't have been more surprised if he'd asked me if I was George Washington. I figured he'd curse me or spit on me, but not that.

Course I was feeling sour anyway, knowing I was having to clean up this mess that I felt was their fault, so I barked right back, "Steal? Take? I'm not stealing anything!" I think it was because I was so mad that I didn't stutter. I was mad about Scrap dying, mad about digging graves, and mad about being called a thief.

He shook his head side to side. He closed his eyes and said, "I don't care what you do on your side. I was just fighting for my family. We don't own no slaves." He was weak but opened his eyes and asked, "If you're not trying to take my land and I'm not trying to take yours, then why am I bout to die?"

I didn't know what to say but just stood there looking at him. All of a sudden I didn't see an enemy soldier, I saw a boy. He didn't look like a demon. He could've been one of your friends. Then I saw why he looked so pale. He held his belly with blood all over his hands. Somehow I didn't even notice that before. It's strange for me to write that, but everybody had some blood on their clothes by then, at least the privates did. As I watched him breathe harder and look weaker, I wasn't mad anymore. Then I heard the sergeant yell my name and knew I had to go. I hated to leave him alone like that. All I could do was shake my head side to side and run towards my company. I never saw that boy again. I don't know his name.

There weren't any undertakers for proper burials, so we did the best we could. Our boys got their own graves. The rebels were heaped in a ditch and we spread dirt over the lot of them, like covering up sick hogs. I'm sure that young rebel I talked to was buried that way. He's somewhere on the field where his family won't ever find him. There's no glory in a mass grave. I never gave much thought about who buried all of the bodies after a battle before, but now I know why it's good to be an officer. I heard one of the rebel generals wrote Grant, asking if he could send some Southern families and troops to bury their dead. Grant let him know we'd taken care of it and by "we" he meant the infantry. We didn't dig just a little bit. For six days, all day long, we buried thousands. I could have turned over a field with all the holes I dug. Course most of the men I buried weren't whole, but like I said, we did the best we could.

Some of the boys took the burying detail as a chance to swap out their clothes. They looked especially for shoes, and given the amount of marching we're doing, I don't blame them. For the most part, men took what they needed. I heard a beat—what we call someone that's extra sorry—from another company took jewelry and money from those lying on the field. And some of the poor souls weren't even dead! When his sergeant got ahold of him he was given extra grave duty plus cleaning up spare pieces. I didn't want any souvenirs. I'd give everything I own to forget the faces. I didn't sleep for three nights. I'd cry if I could, but I'm too tired. I feel like I've been in a dream over the last week.

I just keep doing what I'm told so I'm not punished. Even in my dreams I know not to cross the sergeant.

We've just left Pittsburgh Landing and are trailing the rebels towards Corinth, Mississippi. We're resting now so I figured I'd write a bit. Part of me is afraid I'll forget what happened here, part of me is afraid I won't. Just as we were leaving we passed a little church that the rebel officers had used during the battle. One man from our company who can't read asked me the name of the church. It's Shiloh.

I haven't talked with Jacobs since he saw what I did during the battle. Or what I didn't do. He keeps to himself mostly. I've tried to be friendly to him before but he doesn't respond when you greet him or even ask how he's doing. He just looks straight through you like you're not there. After a while I quit trying to talk with him. I guess some folks just like to be left alone. Not me.

Pray for me Jimmy.

Take care,
Johnny

May 6th, 1862
Pittsburgh Landing, Tennessee

Dear Ms. Elzey,

Thank you for your letter. I was in a big battle down here at Pittsburgh Landing, which you're likely to hear about directly. Our regiment had to help Grant run the rebels out of West Tennessee. The fighting was rough and one of my best friends was killed. I hadn't lost anyone like that before and it's been hard. But I'm fine. I hope the fighting never gets too close to you, cause once it starts there's no telling what's going to happen. I'm looking forward to your quilt. I'm sure I'll need it when the weather turns cold again. Course it's been nothing but wet down here and there's been days when I didn't think the sky would ever be clear again.

I'm from Hardyville, Kentucky. I have an older brother Tom, an older sister Lucy, and a younger brother Jimmy. I help my folks on the farm, raising crops and critters. I love to read, always have. Papa says I'd rather read than eat. Course there's not a lot of books around, but I'll borrow from anyone in our church that has them.

My great-grandfather Notley Gore fought in the Revolutionary War. He died the same year Thomas was born, so I never knew him, but he's a big reason for my joining the army. He fought to make this a country of united states. I'm fighting to keep it that way.

Thanks again for the letter and please write again.

Take care,
John Gore

May 18, 1862

Johnny,

We finally read about the Battle of Pittsburgh Landing in the newspaper, except I also hear folks calling it the Battle of Shiloh, too. Grant said, "There were so many bodies, you could walk across the field and never touch ground." Ma kept asking for the paper after Papa had read it and he told her there wasn't anything in there she didn't already know. She grinned like a mule eating saw briars and said, "Maybe I don't know as much as you think I do." Course normally that'd make Papa smile. It did me. But he didn't. He lowered his voice and told her she shouldn't look at it. But you know her. She would've been Lot's wife for sure. He walked out to the porch as she was reading it. I hadn't read it yet neither, so all I could hear was her saying, "How awful!" "Lord Almighty!" and "Those poor, poor boys!" She said that last one a lot till I went out on the porch with Papa. He was smoking his pipe. He didn't look at me but just said, "I told her not to. Maybe next time I'll try to get her to read it." It would've been funny if it'd been about something else. Then he looked at me and said, "There ain't no use in worrying about Johnny. All we can do is send him little gifts now and then and pray he comes home safe. You're praying, right?" He looked at me like I was about to be in trouble. I told him I was praying a heap and I am. Course I didn't tell him I was praying you come home with a chest full of medals, but then again, he didn't ask.

I know you said your boys weren't causing local folks trouble, but I've heard talk at church of Federal soldiers coming by and taking what they like. It doesn't make sense to me. We follow the law and we're for them. Why would they hurt us?

I'm trying real hard to lay off of Bobby, but it's tough. The devil's been pressing on me to sin. And I want to, I ain't going to lie. I'm trying to be good, honest I am, but I don't know how long I can hold out. Sooner or later he's going to get what he's owed.

Jimmy

May 30th, 1862
Corinth, Mississippi

Dear Jimmy,

We finally took Corinth today, which is about twenty miles southwest of Pittsburgh Landing. I say took, but there wasn't much to it really. There were some scuffles that we thought were leading up to a battle, but they never amounted to anything. Grant's no longer in charge. Instead we have General Halleck, who I've never seen and I haven't talked to anybody who actually has. I know he's as cautious as an old maid and we took a long time to get here from Pittsburgh Landing, setting up defensive works every few yards it seemed, just to make sure we weren't surprised like Grant was. But the rebels were sneaky. They knew they were outnumbered and didn't want to lose more men. We were closing in and they needed more time to get all of their men on trains, since there's a big depot right around Corinth. Their officers ordered three days' rations to be given out, which usually means a long fight. They knew there'd be a couple of theirs switch over to our side and they were right. The traitors said how the rebels were preparing for a battle so Halleck called a meeting with the other shoulder straps to decide what to do. Our scouts reported dozens of cannons around their works, waiting for us to cross the open field. The night before we were ready to attack we could hear trains arriving behind their lines and them screaming their crazy yells. We figured they were cheering a new division arriving to help them fight and we prepared for another big battle.

Except their cannons weren't regular cannons. They were Quaker cannons. They cut logs, painted them black and pointed them towards us. Once we saw they weren't real, we ran over their walls, but it was empty. That's when we thought about the night before. When we figured more rebels were arriving, they were loading on the trains to get out. Most men around the campfire complained about how the cowards should've stayed and fought. For me, I didn't mind. I didn't want to spend another week digging graves. I know I need another chance to be brave, but you can't run a horse all day and all night for long. Sometimes the horse needs to rest.

I don't know why but I don't even have to do anything wrong for the sergeant to pick on me. The other day we were standing in formation and the sergeant asked one of the newer recruits to count out all of the steps in loading a gun. The young private started but then he knew he was missing a step and stopped. He knew how to do it but it's harder when you're just talking about it. Everyone was smiling a little, but the sergeant looked at me and came over and yelled, "Oh, and you think you can do better, Private Gore? Fine, you list all of the steps!" I started and tried but I just couldn't get it out. It took me what seemed like ten minutes to get to number three and finally the sergeant said, "Do you all want to listen to Private Gore stumble through the rest of the steps or get something to eat?" Of course they all said, "Eat!" He dismissed them and then got up in my face and told me to mind my own business. I won't tell you the actual words he used, but let's just say Ma would frown. A lot. I don't know why he picked on me, but he did. Maybe he saw me not speak when Scrap died. I don't remember where he was when it happened. I think he hasn't liked me from the beginning because he felt I could get one of his men hurt. And he was right.

    Take care,
    Johnny

June 16, 1862

Johnny,

I'm glad there wasn't a problem with Corinth. I'm sure your sergeant will take a liking to you once you take out a covey of rebels. He'll come around.

So we were all finished with church and I was talking with George when Bobby comes up and starts asking me when I'm going to bring him some more squirrels. I didn't bite. You would've been proud. I didn't even look at him. But then he started saying, "M-m-m-maybe your older brother J-J-J-Johnny will kill some for m-m-m-me." I couldn't let that go. And didn't. I walked over nice and slow and without saying anything I punched him in his belly as hard as I could. He doubled over and then I got around him and had one arm around his neck and the other arm pulling on my wrist to choke him. He fell down to his knees and I could hear other people making sounds, but no words. I was just thinking about him making fun of you and how I wasn't going to let up. Then I heard a sound I did know, "James Marion Gore!"

I turned around and got a heaping dose of Ma's hand on my face. Bobby stayed on the ground and was choking, but he's fine. Everyone was quiet and stared at me as Ma grabbed me by the ear and took me home. I don't know what hurt my ear worse, the twisting or Ma's preaching. Papa was taking off his belt getting ready to beat me when I finally got a word in and explained why I got so upset. He put his belt back on and told me to go to my room. I could hear them talking and I could tell Papa was on my side. He feels a brother should stand up for his brother. Not that you couldn't have taken Bobby, but you weren't here. Papa never whipped me and nobody's brought it up since.

Bobby hasn't bothered me since the fight. He can't say I jumped him or it wasn't fair since he was teasing me. Now I think we're even. I know you said I should leave him alone but I had to handle it my way.

Jimmy

June 19th, 1862

Dear John Gore,

Well I'm glad you're safe. From the papers and what I've heard at church, the battle you were in sounded awful! I'm so sorry about your friend. I've never lost anybody that young neither. We ain't had any rebels around here, although I wouldn't mind taking aim at a few of them myself. Don't worry about me. I know how to shoot just fine and I ain't afraid to put one of them in my sights. Any of them come around here will regret it.

My Ma has been sick recently. She gets as hot as fire and then sweats like she's been working outside in the heat, but she's been lying in bed all day. She looks real puny like she's lost weight. She takes fits of coughing and sometimes can't hardly breathe. Pa saw Dr. Luke at church and he's supposed to come by sometime this week to check on her.

Winnie's been a big help with Ma sick. She's not a bad cook so long as she keeps her mind on cooking and doesn't start watching a butterfly or something important like that.

I'm including a little pin with my letter. A cross. Now don't you go thinking this is one of those silly good luck charms I hear some men wear. There's no three-legged rabbit hopping around for you to have this. My grandmother gave it to me when I was Winnie's age just before she died. You'll notice it's not like a simple cross because each end has a little rounded cross on it. I always wear it to church every Sunday and I know folks will notice me not wearing it, but this is more important. Now you wear this till you're out of the army, then bring it back. I pray that it keeps you safe.

You look after yourself,
Annie

June 29th, 1862
Huntsville, Alabama

Dear Jimmy,

We're roaming around here in the south trying to catch up to the rebels, I think. To be honest some days it just seems like we're going this way and that. I hope there's a plan behind all of our marching.

I can't blame you for sticking up for me, but I hate that you had to do it. Bobby deserved it, but your temper is going to cause you problems, little brother. If I got into a fight every time someone made fun of how I talk I'd stay black and blue. It's hard when some fool is insulting your kin, but being strong is not just how tough you are in a fight, sometimes it's how long you can hold out. These are dark times. You're going to hear men say all sorts of nonsense to get your hackles up, but you stay still and let it pass. This played out well for you, at least for now, but the next time it may not. These days I can't promise I'll be there when you need me.

I got a pin from Annie. It's a little cross. She's letting me wear it as long as I'm in the army to give me protection. I don't really know how the little pin will stop a bullet, but it won't hurt. Besides, I think she likes me.

Take care,
Johnny

G | **13** | **Ky.**

John J. C. Gore

Pvt., Co. A, 13 Reg't Kentucky Infantry.

Appears on

Company Muster Roll

for May + June, 1862.

Present or absent Present

Stoppage, $ 100 for

Due Gov't, $ 100 for

Remarks:

Book mark:

Chandler

(358)   Copyist

53

CHAPTER FOUR

September 2, 1862

Johnny,

I told you before I'd heard that Federals were stealing from farms around here. Not only that, they're mean. Papa let me go to town with him the other day. He went into the store and I stayed outside with the wagon and Red. Along comes a couple of Federal soldiers, one of them with a black beard and a white stripe just below his bottom lip. I was staring at him and he stopped and looked back at me. He spit out his tobacco juice and just missed my boot. He smelled like kraut that had been set out too long. Finally he asked,

"What you lookin at boy?" I know that I should've just lowered my eyes and not said anything but I couldn't help myself.

"I don't know, but I'm glad it ain't a mirror." To be honest I was pretty pleased with myself. He narrowed his eyes and then smiled. He even laughed a little. He looked me up and down and then acted like he was enjoying something.

"We'll come visit you soon, boy. You and your family. I'll remember you and we'll see if you're so funny then."

He walked off and then few minutes later Papa came out. We headed back home and I hadn't heard from Skunky since. But don't worry, he doesn't scare me. I think he's one of those you just have to look in the eye and not back down from.

Jimmy

September 25th, 1862
Louisville, Kentucky

Dear Jimmy,

I'm praying that what you wrote in the last letter was some story you made up to sound funny. Do you have any idea what's going on? When there's a company or unit set up in a town, they're the law. There's no sheriff or deputy. What they say goes. For heaven's sake, don't insult one of them. Do you even know what rank he was? You'd better pray he doesn't have any bars on his sleeves. If he does, Lord have mercy on you.

That must've happened before Bragg took Munfordville. Our officers got word that the rebel General Bragg was headed north to take Louisville. We'd been trailing Bragg and beat him to Louisville because he stopped in Munfordville for several days. I've walked farther in the last six months then I thought I'd walk my entire life.

All that marching takes a lot out of us, making the evenings when we get to rest feel so good. Course some of the men haven't bathed for a long spell, sometimes I swear it'd turn a hog's stomach. But even on hot September days, we're thankful to have coffee and sugar. The sugar ration comes in the shape of a cone. I keep it wrapped in a rag and whittle off a bit now and again. Sitting around the fire, sipping a cup and telling stories makes me forget about how awful this war can be. Every once in a while we have an early march so for our morning cup we just pour the coffee and sugar in together. We're a frightful sight with black and white teeth! The other day this happened and a couple of boys were smiling at the sergeant and he shook his head.

Later that morning he was standing next to me and whispered, "If you swirl cold water into the pot, the grounds go to the bottom." He was looking straight ahead, but there was nobody but me that could've heard him. I don't know how his trick works, but it does. I told the others and now we don't have to chew our coffee. That's the first time he showed any sign that he may like me, which is a firm step towards promotion.

I bet the early crops are already in. It doesn't look like I'll be breaking any beans this year. You may not believe it, but I miss it. Sitting around in the evening listening to Ma and Papa tell stories feels like a long time ago, but those sure were happy times.

Take care,
Johnny

October 4, 1862

Johnny,

We had plenty of beans this year. I know because I broke twice as many as last year, even if Ma says it ain't so. We've been eating out of the garden except for Sunday dinner when the preacher visits. Ma's been squirreling away some vegetables in the cellar and in the woods on account of the soldiers coming around and helping themselves to whatever they want.

When the rebels came through, several families around here had troops pay them a visit. Sometimes the soldiers ask for food or blankets, sometimes they just take it. But from what I've heard, the rebels have better manners than the Federals. Paul said the rebels came by their house and acted like they were at church. We haven't had any come by here yet, but Papa says if we do that we should give them what they want and don't make trouble. And he said it doesn't matter if they're North or South. Course there's also been talk of people being arrested for giving to the rebels. Someone, and I don't know who, turned in Mr. Crabtree for letting a few rebels spend the night in his barn. He said it wasn't true, but Federal soldiers came and that's the last anybody's seen of him.

Susie died. We couldn't find her so I went and looked over the hill and she was down by the big tree that goes across the creek. She was breathing real hard and couldn't get up. I went and got Papa and he brought his gun. He tried to help her, but said she wasn't acting right and she wasn't going to get better. He said it was wrong to let her suffer so he made it quick.

Jimmy

November 6, 1862
Munfordville, Kentucky

Dear Annie,

We marched all the way to Louisville chasing rebels and keeping them from taking over our state. We were at the Battle of Chaplin Hills and stayed around Perryville for a short spell but now we're back in Munfordville and it looks like we may be here a while. I heard the generals don't like getting into big fights during winter because it's hard to move the wagons and cannons along the roads. I'm not complaining. I've pushed wagons through mud before and it's a mess.

We're keeping a lookout for Morgan. He's as slippery as a catfish. There's several Kentucky regiments that are trying to catch him. Just the other day Pole and I met another private named Wes Robinson. He's from Kentucky with the 10th Infantry. He's tall, around five foot eight, and has a flat nose and a deep voice. Wes is always with Sam Flint, who is shorter and always has plenty to say. Well, a couple of months ago while the pair were on patrol they spied a covey of rebels. Sam wanted to touch a few off, but Wes held him back. The rebels headed to an old lady's house where they told her to give them her money, but she refused. They slapped her around, but she still wouldn't give. Then they decided to lock her in her house and set it on fire. Laughing and yelling, the rebels watched the flames roar and slid into the woods. Wes and Sam rescued the old lady and even though her house burned down, she was fine. Sam said she thanked them for saving her life and then added with a wink, "Those scoundrels never got my money and won't as long as I can kick."

Wes and Sam were watching the house burn when the rebels came back. Finding two Union soldiers and an open door let the rebels know the old lady got the best of them. Seeing how they were outnumbered, Wes and Sam surrendered without a shot. The rebels sure were mad. They locked their Wes and Sam in a little nearby church and set it on fire. Sam says, "Can you believe we were going to die for saving a little old lady from being burned alive?" But the rebels got spooked at something and left, giving Wes enough time to kick out a window.

Right as they finished their story I guess I moved my coat where Sam could see my cross pin. He was laughing and then saw it and asked,

"How'd you get that pin?" I just figured he was admiring it and so without even thinking answered,

"A girl." He jumped to his feet, drew out a knife and said in an angry, shaking voice,

"I'm going to ask you just once more how you got that. And you better answer right." It was like someone had just come up and threw cold water on me. One of my friends, Pole, stood up and explained that I got it from you and that we met while my company was in Campbellsville and that we've been writing letters to each other. Sam simmered down and put away his knife, saying he was your cousin and was going to write you and make sure. He said if he didn't hear back from you he'll hunt me down and gut me. So if you're not too busy, I'd appreciate it if you could write him a letter and explain everything. I really do like the pin, although I thought it was supposed to help protect me.

If you're headed this way for some reason, you may be able to stop by the fort. Or if it's tolerable to you, I might try and visit Campbellsville some time. I'd sure like to see you again, once you let your family know.

Take care,
John

November 21st, 1862
Munfordville

Dear Jimmy,

You may be hearing about rebels being friendly but remember that any one of them would run a blade through me in the blink of an eye. They may act polite now when they're coming to people's doors, but they wouldn't act that way if they saw me. If you knew the rebels like I know the rebels, you wouldn't want anything to do with them.

It was sad to hear about Susie getting sick. I milked her for a few years before you. When I was about seven or eight years old our dog Brandy was chasing her and Susie ran through a field that had just been plowed. That's how she broke her leg. It sure was easier milking a cow with only three good legs. I know it seems strange to be writing you a letter when I'm just outside the town, but I'm not sure when I'll get to leave and I wanted to let you know about the last couple of months.

Well, after we beat Bragg to Louisville, he headed to Frankfort where a confederate governor was being sworn in. Richard Hawes is his name. Can you believe that? Our state with a traitor governor! We hiked to Frankfort but missed Bragg again. Finally, we caught up with him around a small town called Perryville.

Perryville is pretty country, more hilly than here. The fight was a big battle, but my gun stayed cold. We stood in reserve the whole time. I know that doesn't make any sense, but this battle didn't make much sense. See, neither side planned on the battle starting where it did or when it did, but it's been hot and both sides had scouts looking for water. Well, there's a little pond around here and soldiers from each side found it about the same time. And then they started fighting over who gets the water. Both sides fired and then other soldiers heard it and came running and then they joined in. Within a few minutes a spat over some water turned into a full-scale battle with thousands on each side. I heard someone say that General Buell didn't even know the battle had started and sent orders for his batteries to quit firing during his dinner. He thought they were practicing and it annoyed him. This while his troops were dying on the field!

Meanwhile we just stood around looking at each other. By the time we were called in, the fighting was over. And from the look of the field afterwards, they could've used us. What a mess. Actually, the dead don't bother me as much as the wounded that wish they were dead. It's hard to stomach. Before the war I'd never given much thought to all the ways a bullet can tear a body up. Now I don't need to think about it. I've seen it. We're calling it the Battle of Chaplin Hills, but to me it's about like Pittsburgh Landing. We had the field at the end of the day so we can claim a victory, but with so many wounded and killed, it doesn't feel like a win.

We've had a few skirmishes with the rebels since the battle, particularly on the 15th of October. I fired my gun a few times, but I didn't have a chance to do anything, particularly anything to get me noticed by the sergeant or the colonel. Two nights later we had the best night in camp since we left Campbellsville. We captured a few prisoners and—even better—beef.

Our regiment tasted fresh meat for the first time in a long while. We chewed slow and felt like generals as we laughed at jokes, sang some songs, and smoked a leaf or two.

After Chaplin Hills we headed back to Munfordville. At least we're not marching all day. Since everyone's afraid of the Johnnies attacking the railroad, when we first got here we slept in railroad buildings. It wasn't so bad. We cooked outside and slept indoors. After a spell of that we were given a field to set up our camp and have been pretty comfy since. Just the other night we had beef and sweet potatoes followed by fried molasses. Not to mention they just opened up a bakery here so our crackers aren't moldy and dry anymore. I've heard there's about 4,000 troops here.

I don't know when I'll get to come visit. The shoulder straps are getting stricter about letting us go, as some boys haven't come back. We've also had a lot of sickness around here and I don't want to give you any of it. They've had to put men up in hotels, empty buildings, local houses, and just about anywhere they can find a bed. I'll get to see you by and by. It looks like we're going to be here for quite a spell. I heard up to a year to give our regiment a rest since we marched so far over the last several months. We'll be in charge of central Kentucky so we'll have short marches, but not into other states.

Take care,
Johnny

December 20th, 1862

Dear John,

I'm so sorry about Sam. Since I don't have an older brother he's always been protective of me, although he's never threatened anybody with a knife before. I mailed him a letter and told him you were okay and not to be too rough on you. I hadn't seen him for over a year and felt bad that I hadn't written him. The pin came from his grandmother too, which probably didn't help.

I am sending you a couple of jars of jelly, which I hope you'll like. I'd picked out a jar of strawberry but then Winnie said she thought you looked like you favor blackberry, so we packed up both. I'm sorry that you won't be with your family on Christmas. Consider the jelly a gift. I hope by next year this time the war will be over and you'll be home.

Pa made a point to tell me you were welcome to visit here whenever you can. I think he hopes it will keep away the secesh. At our table you can eat all you want. We'll feed you right, none of those sorry vittles the sutlers sell.

I hope that you stay safe and have a Merry Christmas.

Annie

December 23rd, 1862

Dear Jimmy,

Merry Christmas, little brother! It was good to see everyone a few weeks ago. I know I wasn't there very long. Trust me I would have loved to have stayed longer. We didn't get to talk as much as I'd like, but I'm glad we got to visit some. We've been on the move recently, although I don't think we're going to leave the state. I can't write about specifics now because sometimes the rebels open our mail. I'll let you know when I can.

You said you wanted more soldier stories. Last week the sergeant asked for volunteers to carry out a mission from General Grant and I raised my hand along with a few others. I figured it was an order from Grant so it must be important. Perhaps if I did really well then I'd get to meet him. Then we were told that Grant had ordered all the Jews in Kentucky to leave their homes and move North. Of course we were fit to be tied, but there wasn't anything we could do but obey orders. There were a couple of families south of here so a handful of us went and delivered the news. The fathers kept asking us why. They wanted to know what they'd done wrong. All we could say is it was an order by General Grant and they had to move in twenty-four hours. I didn't speak of course. But I was there. I could only look in their eyes for a few seconds and then had to stare straight ahead. As far as I could tell they were just families trying to make a living and not bothering anybody. I never heard any more about it, so I don't know what came of it. I know it left a sour taste in my mouth about volunteering. I didn't sign up for that. And if that's what I have to do to finally get promoted then they can keep it.

I got a letter from Annie and she invited me to eat with her family when I get around Campbellsville again. I thought I was smart by not speaking much when we met but getting to know her through writing letters. I don't think that's going to work at the supper table.

Take care,
     Johnny

| G | 13 | Ky. |

John J. C. Gore

Pvt. , Co. A, 13 Reg't Kentucky Infantry.

Appears on

Company Muster Roll

for From Sept. 6 62 to Jan. 1 , 1863.

Present or absent_____Present_____

Stoppage, $_____100 for _____

Due Gov't, $_____100 for_____

Remarks:_____

Book mark:_____

Chandler

(358)   Copyist.

CHAPTER FIVE

January 2nd, 1863

Johnny,

Well I don't know why you're complaining to me about talking around your girl. If she doesn't like you because you stutter, then find another one. Or better yet, just forget about them.

I don't understand why Grant would want the Jews to leave. I don't see how that will help win the war. Your army just doesn't make sense sometimes.

I know you said the rebels are all a bunch of rotten thieves, but there are some women folk around here who don't feel that way. Somehow the raiders wound up with a pack of women's shoes and went to a few houses, giving away the shoes in return for pies. Now I don't know what they were doing with those shoes in the first place. Mr. Toms said that Morgan's raiders swapped out one of his horses and the one they left turned out a heap better than the one they took. It had to be fed and rested, but once it was healthy it was a fine horse. He was telling me and Papa the story and then winked at me and said in a low voice, "I wonder what they'd swap out for Mrs. Toms?"

I know. I know. The southern half of the country is wrong and you're right. Well, some folks around here aren't so sure.

Jimmy

January 4th, 1863

Dear Annie,

We just passed through Campbellsville after the raid. In fact, we're chasing Morgan right now. We've been marching with barely any time to rest or eat, so the colonel gave us a spell. I figured I'd write you a quick letter just to ask how you've been. I wish I could've come to your farm and made sure you and your family were okay, but I have to follow orders. By the way, that was awful good jelly. Winnie was right!

One more thing. And this is hard to write. I didn't talk much when you helped carry one of the boxes and so I don't know that you noticed, but sometimes I stutter. Not all the time, but when I get nervous. I rarely stutter at home or when I'm around Pole here. But when the sergeant calls on me my tongue starts acting up and I can't always control it. I feel like I have to tell you because I don't want you to be embarrassed if I ever get to meet your folks and then I have trouble talking. I know some girls don't want to be around a boy that can't speak well. I understand. People have made fun of me my whole life because of the way I talk. I deal with it because it's my problem, but if I'm at your dinner table, it will be your problem too.

If you don't think it'd be a good idea for me to come visit or even keep writing you, then this may be my last letter. If you're still interested in me coming to visit, then I'll look forward to hearing from you. Either way, the sooner the better.

Take care,
John

January 12th, 1863

Dear Jimmy,

You'll be happy to know I did write the girl and tell her about my stuttering. She may never write me again, which I know you'd like, but at least I don't have to worry about it anymore. It's good that I can't go and get that letter and take it back.

I couldn't write it out in my last letter, but just before Christmas there was talk about Morgan coming to destroy the Green River bridge and the railroad depot, which is of course where we're at. I couldn't write it because sometimes the rebels tear open everyone's mail to see if they can find us. Anyway, we got word he went through Glasgow and was headed for us, so Christmas day and night we stayed around the bridge ready for a fight. We stood real quiet, hiding in a barn the whole night just looking at the walls. Every once in a while we'd hear something and men would nod their heads like we were going to start shooting any minute. But the fighting never came. It turns out Morgan never planned on attacking the Green River bridge, he was headed to Elizabethtown to tear up the trestles there. Morgan and his raiders tore up the track and tied the rails into bows. They do that by heating up the rails and bending them around trees so we have to lay down new ones. They're just plain ornery. Those polite, noble rebels you hear so much about.

But don't think we were just sitting around wondering what to do. Colonel John Harlan took us and some other regiments and chased the raiders down. The 13th Kentucky is now led by Colonel William Hobson

(General Hobson's nephew). We did finally catch up with the rebels at the mouth of Beech Fork on the Rolling Fork River. Our cannons fired on them and I think did some damage, but they got away over the bridge. Seeing how we'd marched over forty miles in thirty hours, we let them go, which was probably for the best. We were so tired we wouldn't have been any count in a fight anyway.

Then on December 31st they entered Campbellsville. The raiders tore up the post office there, too. Mr. Redman, who owns the Golden Horse Tavern, lost a couple of thousand dollars in leather that the rebels stole as Morgan set up headquarters there. Just about everybody in town lost something, and some lost everything. There wasn't a decent horse left in the city. Then, to really tear the hide from all the townsfolk, the rebels decided they didn't want to leave any food for Federal Union soldiers. So they piled up a mountain of bacon, molasses, and crackers in the city and set it on fire. Here some of the people didn't have much food left after the rebels stole it and then they burnt up pounds and pounds of it right in front of them. The fire was still burning when we arrived. I heard one old lady say about Morgan, "If I put him in a sack and shook it up, I don't know what end would come out first!" Course I wanted to go and find Annie and her family, but I couldn't. Orders are orders.

I don't know where we're going to be next as we're trailing Morgan.

Take care,
Johnny

January 14th, 1863

Dear John,

I know you were trying to be sweet by telling me about your stuttering, at least that's what I keep telling myself. Did you really think I didn't notice? Now if you told me you wanted to be a preacher, then you might need to check with the Lord. Cause I don't think that's your gift. But aside from that, I don't mind. And don't you worry about my folks. My Pa mumbles half the time anyway, especially when he's giving directions on chores he wants done. He likes to turn his head away from you while he's mumbling about something to do and then when he turns back to you he say in a stern voice, "And I want that done by the time I get back." So don't pay him any mind and Ma won't mind either. You've got plenty to worry about with catching Morgan. Don't you waste any time fretting about us. You're welcome here whenever you get a chance.

Ma was down in her back again yesterday. She says it feels like her leg's on fire and she can't get the pain out. She'll cry from the pain and there ain't no way for her to get comfortable. She'll get these spells and it sometimes lasts for a couple of weeks before it works itself out. We'll have the doctor come over and he'll give her medicine but it doesn't help. I feel sorry for her, but when she's down we have to wait on her hand and foot. The problem is, other than her complaining, she doesn't look sick.

I hope to see you soon,
Annie

January 27th, 1863

Dear John,

    I know I just wrote you a letter but I feel that I have to tell someone about last week. It's been the worst several days of my life.

    It was cold on January 20th, the coldest day I ever remembered. My folks, Winnie, and myself were all inside around the fire after eating dinner. Even though it was the middle of the day, the sky was gray and it was hard to tell exactly where the sun was. We were sitting around listening to Ma tell a story and then Winnie turned her head and asked, "Did you hear that?" Just after she said it the door was kicked open and in came three rebel soldiers. These weren't the men in the hats with large plumes and fancy beards. These men were common, dirty, and mean. They weren't with Morgan's original group, but they were rebels for sure. One of them picked up Winnie and put a gun to her head and then made Pa give them money. Another one went into the kitchen with a sack and started stealing food. Ma went in and tried to stop him, but he pushed her down and then her back started hurting her so she couldn't move. The man holding Winnie took her outside and Pa went with them. I saw Ma on the floor crying and helped get her up to the bed. I was getting a towel to put on her forehead. She was staring out the window and then cried, "Oh no, the barn!" I looked outside and our barn was covered in flames. I looked at Ma and she said, "Go! Help him!"

    I ran outside and saw the rebels riding off with a large sack of our food. Then I started running to Pa who was on the ground with blood running from his head. I got close to him and asked, "Are you okay? Where's Winnie?" He pointed and said in a hoarse voice, "Barn." I spun around and saw her deep in the barn, lying on the floor. Not moving. She must've been knocked down by one of the mules. As I stepped to the barn, the top level fell. Pa was on his feet. We both knew that the bottom was going to fall any second. He started to go in, but I held him back. I just remember screaming and crying, "No Pa, please don't go! You'll die!" I only held him for a couple of seconds and then the barn collapsed. We both fell down and wept. I don't know how long we sat there apart, until he finally came over and put his arm around me and cried some more. After a spell he went inside and told Ma. I don't remember the rest of the day. I don't rightly know many of the details over the next few days. But I remember the box. That cold box that they put Winnie in. Poor little Winnie.

I know that God rules the heavens and the Earth. I know that He does everything for a reason. But I'll never know why he let my baby sister die.

Please pray for me and my family. I hope you can still read this letter. I know the ink is running. I'm sorry. I tried but I can't think of her without crying.

Look after yourself and get those rebels.

Annie

January 29, 1863

Johnny,

I read your letter about how Morgan burned up Campbellsville, but from what I heard, they started it. Before the war, Campbellsville arrested him for selling pants to the rebels. Can you believe it? Pants. It was after that arrest he formed his company and started fighting against the North. Morgan always held a grudge against Campbellsville for jailing him and was just waiting for a chance to get back. I guess he figured they had it coming.

Now let me tell you what happened to us last week. It was really cold, like freeze your nose hairs cold. I was outside checking on the horses when I saw four riders coming down our lane. It was dusk so I couldn't make out who they were until they got close. I didn't try and run for it, so I just kept walking towards the house and before I got there they surrounded me.

"Well, well, well. Looky here boys! Why this is the boy I saw in town who was talking about how pretty I was. Weren't you, boy?" I knew by the sound of his voice it was Skunky, whatever his name is. I looked up at him but didn't say anything.

"What's a matter, boy? You were all ready to talk the other day." He jumped down off his horse and started coming towards me. His rotten cabbage smell hit me before he got too close. I stood my ground. He was taller than me, probably as tall as you, but fatter.

"You listen here, boy. We can't stay for now, but we'll be back. And when we do we'll help ourselves to whatever we want. You don't have much to say now, do you? That's what I thought." As he said the last part he pushed his finger on my chest and pushed me back a little. He jumped back on his horse.

"See that boys, he's got some fire in his eyes. This is going to be fun." They rode off. It didn't last very long and so I went back inside. Ma and Papa never heard or seen anything so I didn't say anything to them. That's your great Federal army. By the way, he has three stripes on his sleeve with a diamond on top, whatever that means.

You should be proud of me for not talking back to him. I didn't say a word. But I looked him in the eye and I didn't look away. He knows I'm not scared. He'll be back, but I ain't gonna lose sleep over Skunky.

Jimmy

February 12, 1863

Dear Annie,

Reading your letter felt like somebody hit me in the stomach with a rifle. I'm so sorry for Winnie. She was such as sweet little girl. Before the war I never gave any thought to people getting hurt who weren't actually fighting, but I've seen and heard plenty of it now. I'll always remember her bright blue eyes and her smile.

It wasn't supposed to be like this. The war, I mean. It's nothing like how I thought it would be. It should've been men lining up on battlefields, marching towards one another, shooting on command and then receiving medals of glory. Watching my friend die in that dirty, smelly, bloody field was horrible. And hearing how Winnie died is worse.

How I wish my regiment had been there when those rebels showed up. It's hard since Morgan and his regiment are on horseback and we're on foot. How I wish we could meet them in an open field but of course Morgan won't allow it. Since Morgan is roaming all over Kentucky, so are we.

I don't know what to say other than I'm sorry. I'll pray for you and your family. And you can be sure that I'll do everything I can to help catch Morgan and his band. Don't worry, when we get him, he'll pay.

Take care,
John

February 18th, 1863

Dear Jimmy,

Little brother, how I wish I could be there to talk with you face to face. I want you to look me in the eyes and see my concern. I'd like you to hear the worry in my voice. The Federal soldier that you've angered is a first sergeant. Do you have any idea what this means and what he can do? If he has reason to believe you're with the South he can bring a regiment to our house, take everything, and burn it to the ground. This isn't a game. If he shows up again then you need to address him as "Sergeant" and give him whatever he wants. Don't talk back to him and don't stare him down. You know that will just make him mad.

And I don't know what you mean by "my army." I'm a private in the army of the United States of America, the same army our great-grandfather served in to form our country. This is your army too, not the bunch of traitors wearing gray. Speaking of the rebels, let me tell you what kind of people they are. Annie's farm was hit by a group of rebels. They stole food, burned up their barn, and Annie's little sister Winnie was in the barn when it fell. Winnie was younger than you, around ten years old. Annie's Pa couldn't fight back. There was no reason to burn down their barn except meanness. There's the rebel army for you.

I know you don't like being pushed around and you've been told your whole life not to let anyone run all over you, but I'm telling you now, this is different. Common folk are getting killed just like soldiers. What's important is that our family survives. That you survive.

A petty squabble with a mean sergeant won't matter once this is all over.

Think about this.

Take care,
Johnny

February 22, 1863

Dear Annie,

I know I didn't write that long ago, but I wanted to let you know about what we've been doing. We haven't caught Morgan yet, but it's not from a lack of trying. We've come close, sometimes just minutes behind him, but he always manages to slip away. After I read about Winnie dying, I've had a terrible itch to get into a fight with a rebel. Any rebel. We've had some men who had kin in Campbellsville and they said even if Morgan threw up his hands, they'd still shoot. I hope I wouldn't do that.

A couple of weeks ago, we were marching along with General Hobson on a rumor about Morgan's whereabouts. All of a sudden, a Union soldier on horseback jumped out of the woods and headed straight to the general. We knew some of Morgan's men dressed as Union soldiers from time to time, so a couple of boys blocked him, but he was determined. He barked, "I need to see our general now! It's urgent!" There wasn't any doubt in his voice and everybody let him pass. He saluted General Hobson and the two talked for a couple of minutes. Pole and I happened to be close to the general at the time and we'd never seen anything like it. General Hobson stopped his horse and started chuckling. Then he shook his head and looked in our direction and said, "Seize him." The rebel thought we were Morgan's company dressed as Union soldiers. He was warning General Hobson about the nearby Union army. They out-sneaked themselves.

The rebel lieutenant didn't offer much useful information once he was found out. He was ordered to strip off the uniform and walk with his hands tied. Nobody beat him on the general's orders, but we had plenty to say about how smart he was. He was later used to trade for a Union officer. Course they don't trade for common soldiers. We get shipped off to prisons. I haven't ever talked to a private who's escaped or been in a prison, so I don't know what it's like.

I think about you a lot. I wish I could've been there when they came to your farm. Now I wish I could be at your place and also my home. My brother Jimmy has gotten on the bad side of a sergeant stationed around Munfordville and I'm afraid of how the sergeant may respond. Jimmy doesn't understand what soldiers can do, Federal or rebel. I told him about your house and Winnie, but I don't think he believes me. He's fifteen going on sixteen and walks around like a banty rooster.

It helps me to write you. Sometimes I like to be alone in my tent writing my letter when everyone else is sitting around the campfire. Even if Pole is in the tent too and he's quiet. He writes his folks almost every week. We get issued beeswax candles every month. What most boys use, and what I used to use, was my bayonet stuck in the ground and put the candle in the part that attaches to the gun. But Pole and I bought a little wooden box with a mirror in the back. We can sit the candle in there and it lights up the tent just fine. It's not much fun to carry when we march, so we take turns packing it.

We were supposed to be stationed in Munfordville for a long spell to give us rest but we've done nothing but march for the last few months. We're finally back at the Munfordville camp for a week or so and then will likely be sent after Morgan again. I'm not saying this to complain but to let you know why I haven't visited you recently. As soon as I can I'll be in Campbellsville.

I hope you don't mind, but I wrote you a couple of lines of poetry to cheer you up. Let me know what you think.

> Sure as the rats run round the rafter,
> I long again to hear your laughter.

Take care,
    John

| G | 13 | Ky. |

Jas. J. C. Gore

Pvt., Co. A, 13 Reg't Kentucky Infantry.

Appears on

Company Muster Roll

for Jan. & Feb. , 186 3.

Present or absent Present

Stoppage, $ 100 for

Due Gov't, $ 100 for

Remarks:

Book mark:

Chandler

Copyist.

(358)

CHAPTER SIX

March 2, 1863

Johnny,

Ma and Papa say you look about the same, maybe a little thinner. They got word from the Allen's that your regiment was back in Munfordville. Ma says it was hard for her to see you in a soldier's uniform with all those other men. She said she could look in your eyes and still see her little boy. Course she wouldn't ever say that in front of you. But you know how she talks like that.

We should be starting to plant in a week or two. As soon as we get a couple of dry days we'll set out the early crops. We're hoping we don't have a late snow. Papa says every time he waits it don't snow and whenever he plants early it does. Ma told him to plant a little piece so we'll just get a frost. He smiled and then a minute or two later even laughed a bit. He's worried because if we have gardens full of food then we'll get hungry soldiers stopping by. We don't want them to take all our food, but what else are we to do? We either starve and nobody comes around or have food to eat and worry about soldiers from either side taking it. So we're just going to go ahead and squirrel away what we can.

Don't worry about me. I know what to do when Skunky comes around again. I'll be good and won't even talk back. You'll see.

I'm sorry about your friend's sister.

Jimmy

March 10, 1863

Dear John,

Well, I wish you would've been here when I read your letter. I ain't ever had a boy write me poetry before, and what do you write about? Flowers? No. Grass, trees, hills? No. You write about rats. Thinking about it made me laugh so hard I could barely breathe.

Thanks for letting me know about your chasing Morgan. I agree it wouldn't be right to shoot him if he surrenders, no matter how much you may want to. And Winnie wouldn't want that neither. But I hope you catch him and his pack of wolves. Last Sunday our preacher spoke on Ecclesiastes 7:14, "In the day of prosperity be joyful, but in the day of adversity consider: God also hath set the one over against the other, to the end that man should find nothing after him." I believe in my head that God makes the good and the bad, but I'm having a hard time making my heart believe it. It just hurts too much. I'm praying. That's about all I can do.

I hate going to church now, not because I don't like the preacher, but it's some of the old folks. The old women start crying as soon as they see me, so I can't help but feel sad when all of these weepy women come around me. And the men aren't much better. "Well, you're lucky they didn't set your house on fire with you in it. You sure were lucky." Except I don't feel lucky. Sometimes I wonder why God let me live and Winnie die. I wasn't any better than her. Fact is, she was the happiest little girl I've ever known. Folks have said all sorts of things like, "She's in heaven now singing with the angels so you should be glad for her." Maybe I should, but I'm not. I don't know why, but there ain't nothing that anybody says that helps.

I hope when this is all over those rebels pay. Lord forgive me, I want them to pay. I'm trying not to let my heart get filled with hate. There's one woman at church who lost her only child at Shiloh. She still wears black every day and she ain't smiled since. I don't know that she'll ever smile again. I know Winnie wouldn't want me to be like that and that's what I keep telling myself.

I understand that you're moving around a lot. Just let me know when you might be coming to Campbellsville. I'll make sure and set a place for you at the table. I'd like to see you. My folks would like to see you, too. I know at first Ma wasn't too sure about me writing to a solider, but since you're Federal, she's taken a liking to you.

Look after yourself,
Annie

March 16th, 1863
Munfordville, Ky

Dear Annie,

I'm sorry you're still struggling. I wish I knew something clever to write. I don't know except to keep praying. And don't lose hope.

I've heard we're going to be leaving camp in a couple of days and I've heard we won't be leaving camp for a couple of months, so I don't know. We'll sometimes take short marches to towns ten miles away when we hear of Morgan or other rebels raiding a town but I haven't fired on anyone for a long time.

Back when I was at Camp Andy Johnson around Campbellsville, we had folks come to the camp to feel safe. General Hobson's family came and stayed for a while and their slaves came too. We had runaway slaves show up from time to time when we were first in camp, but the law said that we couldn't let them stay. According to General Hobson, we were not there to take slaves from their owners but "to sustain the best government on Earth." The runaways didn't understand and looked sad when we told them, but some of us would give them a little hardtack and water and told them to keep going north. Other soldiers would tease them, which seemed especially cruel.

Once I joined the army, I saw a chance to get respect if I could get a promotion or a medal. I had hoped to perform a brave act at Shiloh, but it didn't work out. I wasn't a coward. I did my duty, but nothing that would make me stand above the rest of the regiment. I always thought the war would have lots of battles, but Shiloh has been the only major battle our regiment has fought. So I've been volunteering for extra picket duty. Pole and most of the others think I've lost what little sense I had, but I needed more chances.

This particular night a few weeks ago was Pole's regular night to be on picket so we were on together. We both heard something running towards us through the brush and a young slave, probably about my age, came out of the woods. As soon as he saw us, he came a few yards short and stopped. He bent over with his hands on his knees. He kept saying, "I's so glad I made it" over and over again. Pole and I were just looking at him for a spell before I said, "Let's get him some bread and water. He can spend the night next to our tent and then leave in the morning." Pole agreed, so we took him in. Normally if we find anything on picket then one of us has to run back and tell a sergeant and then run into camp. Since he wasn't a rebel, we just let him stay with us until our picket was up.

We went to our sergeant and as soon as he saw the three of us his face took on the same look as when we first started drilling and everybody was going in the wrong direction. Just as we were getting close enough to speak and were thinking of what we were going to say he interrupted us, "He's your responsibility if he stays, you understand." We nodded and headed to our tent. Like me, Pole had never talked to a slave before, so we were both curious and wanted to ask him lots of questions.

First we gave him some hardtack and water. Now either one of us would gladly give him some hardtack, as we eat it more out of necessity to stay alive rather than for any sort of enjoyment. But letting him drink from our canteen was a little different. Pole and I both looked at each other for a few seconds to see who would offer the canteen. Finally I did. Later, Pole and I both felt bad about that. After we gave him some food and water we started asking questions.

His name is Isaac. He didn't know his last name. He'd never known his mother or his father. He was told that his mother had many children because she had them so easy. She was given a dress for each child but she died from childbirth when he was only a few years old. Isaac lived in South Carolina until a year ago. He had worked on a plantation but had tried to escape. Before the war he might've been killed, but with the war on, his owner needed to sell him to make some money. Isaac was sold to a man in Tennessee and had been there for the last year but escaped a couple of weeks ago. He's been heading north and thought he'd be free when he reached us, but we had to tell him Kentucky was still not a free state.

The next morning, once it was light, I could tell Isaac was staring at me, studying my face. Finally I looked at him and asked, "What the matter?" He immediately looked at his feet and slumped. He apologized and said I just reminded him of one of his young masters. He asked if I had any kin in South Carolina. I told him I didn't. We don't have any relatives in South Carolina that I know of. I don't want to write and ask Papa in a letter because I haven't been writing them much lately and it would be strange for that to be the purpose of the letter. I'll get Jimmy to ask. He won't mind.

Take care,
John

March 18, 1863
Munfordville, Ky

Dear Jimmy,

Life in camp's been pretty slow. We're finally getting to rest some. We have daily inspection by the sergeant and drill for a hour once a day but that's about it. We haven't had any real fighting, for that we're waiting on dry roads. The army has finally figured out there's no use trying to push wagons through mud, so the generals take time off and plan. I hope they'll have better luck this year.

With idle hands there are plenty of bluff games plus dice, checkers, and dominoes. I have to be careful about who I play with, to make sure they know I stutter. Nothing's worse than when we're playing a game and then I stutter when it's getting serious and one of them starts making fun of me. He acts like he's being clever, like I've never heard it before. The other day a couple of boys wanted to play bluff with Pole and myself. I was asking for a couple of cards and my tongue got stuck. I didn't look the other boys in the eyes and Pole just said, "Two." I could see out of the corner of my eye Pole shaking his head back and forth, letting them know not to press it. They dropped it and we didn't have an argument. Pole's the best friend I've ever had. Without the war I never would have met him.

By the way, we were telling stories about our kin and it occurred to me, I'm not for sure where Notley went after the war. I figured he went to Kentucky, which is where granddaddy was born. But could you ask Papa just to make sure? I was just curious.

Take care,
Johnny

March 28, 1863

Johnny,

Brother, I hope you're last few days have been better than ours. We're okay. I mean, nobody's dead. But we had a visit that I expect I won't be forgetting anytime soon. I've been so mad I can hardly think.

A week ago we were just finishing dinner. I remember I was getting an extra piece of cornbread when I heard Joe barking. The three of us looked at each other and I dropped my food and ran to the door with Ma and Papa right behind me. We could see about a dozen troops on horseback riding up our road. Now I could see they were Union, but I knew that sometimes rebels wear blue too. I stood there looking at them while Ma walked outside.

As they rode up she said, "Good day gentleman, what can we do for you?"

They didn't speak but rode around our house. Finally one got off his horse and went to our pen with the two hogs. One would dress 200 and the other 250. They started to take the bigger one.

Ma asked, "Wait, why are you stealing our best hog?"

I could hear the a soldier say, "You secesh are lucky we don't take everything you own and burn down your house. It's what you deserve!"

I could tell by her voice that Ma was shook. She said, "Secesh? Why I've got a boy with the 13th Kentucky. His name is John Gore and he was at Pittsburg Landing. They've been marching around Kentucky trying to catch Morgan. We're Union."

He laughed at her. "Sure you are. That's what all you secesh say and then you try to blow up our railroads and bridges. And I don't want any back talk, you hear!"

I could tell the soldier was walking towards the front porch and was coming up the steps. It was Skunky. I think even if I didn't see his beard I could smell him. I swear I don't know how he always smells like burnt cabbage. I was standing in the doorway so Skunky couldn't see me, but when I saw him approach Ma then I stepped out and he saw me.

Then one of the officers on a horse yelled, "Stop! Let her be sergeant! Take the animal and let's go."

Then Sergeant Skunk saw me. He started smiling. Not a jolly smile, but because he saw how he was going to get revenge on me. He'd been chewing tobacco and had had it in his teeth and some of the spit didn't clear his beard.

"Oh no sir! I won't hit the lady, but I'd like to teach her boy here a lesson or two. C'mon lieutenant, let me have just a couple of good licks. He's been disrespectful to Federal soldiers. Why, for all I know he's the one tearing up the rail tracks." I was losing my temper and quick. I couldn't help but talk back.

"Tear up the tracks? Why you no count piece of—"

"Enough!" barked the lieutenant who was rubbing his head with his right hand like he was pushing his eyes deep into his skull.

"Sergeant, get the animal and let's go. Thank you folks for supporting your country."

We just stood there and then Ma sat down on the front steps and cried. I don't remember the last time I'd seen her cry like that. She kept looking at Papa saying, "But we're not secesh. Why'd they treat us that way?" He sat down and put his arm around her. I stood there and didn't know what to do. Seeing her hurt like that made me want to go get that sergeant. He wasn't much bigger than me. I'd like to get working on him and not let up. I'd teach him what a Kentucky boy can do.

They asked me what the sergeant meant by me disrespecting him. I told them that I was in town and looked at him. He talked to me and I didn't say anything back. They told me to do whatever he says from now on. But there ain't no way I can let everything go. I thought I was doing good to not get into a fight with him when he started towards Ma.

I asked Papa about Granddaddy. He said that after the Great War, Notley went down to South Carolina and had nine kids, Granddaddy was the third. He didn't know when exactly, but Granddaddy moved to Kentucky and Notley came too. Papa didn't really know why Granddaddy left South Carolina but said that he never remembered him going back or even writing his kin there. Have you fought any rebels from South Carolina? Course if you meet any of our folks from down there it's probably best you don't know.

And to poor salt on a wound, Joe went missing a couple of days ago and this morning I found him dead behind the barn. He was old but I loved that old rascal and I know you did too. Papa had to bury him down by the creek near the lower field. I couldn't do it.

Jimmy

April 10th, 1863
Munfordville, KY

Annie,

Well, my family had a visit from soldiers, but they weren't wearing gray. They accused my folks of being rebel spies and took one of our hogs. Jimmy said he and my folks were upset, especially being called traitors when I'm out here fighting. I'm afraid my little brother is starting to like the rebels, as he only sees them being nice to the people around Hardyville while our troops are acting ugly. It's hard to explain how the rebels are wrong and we're right when he sees men in blue stealing and being mean. I don't know what I'd do if he joined the other side. I'm afraid I'm losing him. I'd die for my brother, and if needed I'd kill to save his life. I hope I never have to choose between my brother and my country. They'd shoot me for treason.

Jimmy also told me that my Granddaddy had eight siblings in South Carolina. As soon as I read the letter I found Isaac and asked him the name of his young Master, which he said was "Robert Go."

I asked him slowly, "Are you saying Robert Gore?" He looked at me puzzled and then replied, "Yes sir, that's what I sayin, Robert Go."

I felt like someone took a bellows and sucked the life out of me. I've never been against slavery but I wasn't for it either. Since we never owned slaves and didn't really know anyone with slaves I just felt like it didn't affect me. We've kept Isaac around for a while now and he's really not any trouble. In fact, he can cook a lot better than Pole or myself. He stank so bad we made him wash himself and his clothes. When he took off his shirt all we could do was stare. I'd never seen the like of the scars on his back. It was scars on top of scars. I can't imagine what he's been through. I also can't imagine my own kin doing this to him, but I know it's likely true. There's so many different problems going on now that I don't understand and don't know what's right or wrong. But I know slavery is wrong.

So under all those heavy clouds I think about coming to Campbellsville and seeing you. That always puts a smile on my face. And with everything going on, I need a smile now and then. If I'd have known we were going to be staying in Munfordville this whole time I would've already been to visit you. Maybe I'll get word that we're going to be here another month or two and then they'll let me leave.

Okay, so let me try another poem.

> The lilies are sweet and so are the pinks,
> but you are the fairest of all I think.

Take care,
John

April 15th, 1863

Jimmy,

Little brother, reading your letter made me feel like I'd marched all day and all night. I know what Uncle Hestor means when he says, "They done used me up." It's hard for me to be here when I read what you went through.

Papa's right, it could've been a lot worse. He's also right not to fight them, no matter how mad you get. If you attack a soldier they can arrest you and send you off to a prison camp. Or they could just shoot you. And there's some guys ornery enough to do it. I mean it. If they come around again just do what they say. Remember what Papa says about a strange dog? Don't look it in the eye. Well, don't look any of the soldiers in the eye either, especially that sergeant. He'll take it as a challenge. If he does come back then I need you to let me know what regiment and company he's with, at least what state he's from. I've been on the lookout for him but I haven't seen him. There's thousands of us around here and regiments come and go. I understand you weren't having a friendly chat but if you find out what state he's from and regiment it would really help. Better yet, find out his name. His real name.

Don't let one bad apple spoil your feelings towards Federal soldiers. We're not all like that sergeant. The Federal army is trying to keep law and order in the land. It's up to us to keep the trains running to towns like Munfordville. But every time we turn around the rebels are destroying the railroads. And I tell you something else, they're wrong on slavery. Slaves aren't animals. They're people.

I'm looking to visit Campbellsville in a couple of weeks. I have to get the courage up to write Annie and ask. I'm scared of sitting around the table with her folks looking at me and asking me questions. I'd rather be in a battle with the rebels then the thought of them asking a question and then two minutes of me hissing, trying to get a word out. I've been telling her I want to visit and I do. But I also have this fear I might ruin what has been so good.

That's too bad about Joe. He was a good dog.

Pray for me brother as I pray for you.

Take care,
Johnny

April 26, 1863

Dear Annie,

I know this isn't much notice, but I hope to be in Campbellsville the first week of May for a day or two. I'd like to call on you if you'll accept. I'll be coming by your farm, but I wanted to let you know in advance.

I'm really looking forward to seeing you again,

John

P.S. You may want to warn your folks that I don't talk much. It's not that I have bad manners. I'm just quiet. Thanks.

G | 13 | Ky.

John J. C. Gore

Pvt., Co. A, 13 Reg't Kentucky Infantry.

Appears on

Company Muster Roll

for Mar. & Apr., 186 3.

Present or absent. Present.

Stoppage, $ 100 for

Due Gov't, $ 100 for

Remarks:

Book mark:

Easterling

(358) Copyist.

CHAPTER SEVEN

May 2nd, 1863

Dear Johnny,

I read your letter a couple of times. Maybe you're right. It's not that I'm looking for a fight. Honest I'm not. I've been told my whole life not to back down to anybody, so I'm not. I've seen Papa be quiet before, but I ain't ever seen him look at the ground when another man was talking to him. When I see someone come onto our land and push around Ma and Papa it makes my eyes wide and I get testy. I guess I'll just have to think of Skunky like eating the fat with the lean. Swallow the fat with a biscuit and forget about it.

A couple of weeks ago we were plowing the field nearest the road and a stray dog came up. Since Joe died, Papa said I could keep him if he didn't bite and he'd come to me. He's a white and brown pointer, strong and muscular, but boy is he ugly. He has a snaggletooth sticking out on the left bottom corner when he smiles. I named him Fiddler. Old Fiddler's a good dog, but he's a little light on brains. A couple of days ago I was walking near the pond below the tobacco barn and Fiddler fell in. I always thought all dogs could swim, but I guess Fiddler never learnt. Papa had just come out of the barn and saw Fiddler in the water and asked me what I thought was going to happen. He said unless I went in the pond the dog would drown. I just hope Fiddler doesn't decide to learn how to swim next January.

I'll pray for you, but not for your courting.

Jimmy

May 14th, 1863
Lebanon, Ky

Dear Jimmy,

I know you'd rather read about me shooting rebels but there hasn't been much fighting and the drilling is the same. We marched to Lebanon on the rumor Morgan was here but I haven't seen any sign of him. Since these are letters that I'm going to read when I'm older, I'm going to write about what I want. And I just had the best weekend of my life.

I went to Campbellsville and saw Annie. We got to spend the whole day together. I let her do most of the talking but even when I did talk I didn't stutter too much. She's so fun to be around I think I smiled all day. And she smells like honeysuckle that's just bloomed. We sat on her porch in a couple of large green chairs and talked. We even forgot to eat dinner. Annie and her ma cooked fried chicken with biscuits and gravy and I swear it was the best I've had in two years (Ma didn't cook it when I was home). I think Annie may have been showing off a bit with her fried chicken. And I loved every bite. While they were cooking I was talking with her pa, who is quiet but friendly. He knew I didn't like to talk much so he asked me questions I could nod my head to answer. But during dinner her ma asked me several questions at once and then I'd start hissing trying to start a word. I was getting stuck and I could feel the sweat on my brow and I was getting flushed. You have no idea what it's like to be twenty-one years old unable to answer a simple question. Not only that, her ma talked slowly and loudly to me.

Then her pa spoke up and asked Annie if he'd told her about seeing a group of federal soldiers the other day. He said he was coming from town and saw a covey of soldiers working along the L & N Railroad, except they weren't working. There were lying down under a tree talking and laughing. He was coming right past them so he stopped and asked how the track was coming. They said, "Fine, just fine. We just saw a secesh rabbit go in this hole so we're waiting till it comes out to let him have it."

He asked, "How'd you know the rabbit's secesh?"

The soldier said with a wink, "Easy. He's wearing gray."

Writing it now doesn't seem very funny, but when he told the story it was quiet for maybe ten seconds and then Annie snickered, then I laughed, then we starting laughing so hard we weren't very polite. I guess I'd been so nervous that when I really started laughing I got the nerves out of my system. Anyway, her ma didn't ask me more questions after that and when her pa asked me questions, I didn't stutter much. It turned out to be a wonderful time.

I know you don't care about courting, but just you wait, someday you'll want to enjoy the best part of life.

I look forward to meeting Fiddler the next time I'm home.

Take care,
Johnny

May 21, 1863

Dear Annie,

I wanted to thank you again for letting me visit you and your family. I'm still thinking about the fried chicken and gravy. It's the best I've had. Course I'd been just as happy to just sit on the porch and talk with you as eat, even the fried chicken. I enjoyed getting to talk with your folks, especially your pa. I think he likes me. I understand he mainly likes me because I'm fighting the rebels but that's okay. I'm just glad he didn't pull a gun on me and tell me to leave. Spending the day with you was the best day of my life. If I didn't have my uniform on, I'd have forgotten all about the war. I want to thank you for that too. It means so much to think about life outside of soldiering.

I need to let you know I have feelings for you. And I hope you have feelings for me too.

Oh, and here goes another try at poetry.

> The pine is tall and the cedar is small.
> You are my choice among them all.

Take care,
John

May 25, 1864

Dear Johnny,

Mr. Charlie came to visit the other day. I always like to see him and hear his stories. Course Ma says he lies so much that he doesn't know what the truth is any more, but I don't care. I asked him about hunting and trapping. He says he caught seventy foxes between here and Horse Cave. He left the rest to breed for next year. Papa couldn't help but laugh. Mr. Charlie then went on to say he'd hit a quail one time walking away and shot over his shoulder without looking. He's a card.

We had other visitors last week. We were eating supper and the wind was blowing real hard, so we couldn't hear anything. All of a sudden there was a knock at the door. Papa got up and in walks three men with big hats and moustaches. They were secesh cavalry. I don't know if they were passing through or if they were being chased by some Federals. The tallest one did the talking. He took off his hat and looked at Papa and said, "Evening." Then he looked at Ma and said, "Ma'am. We need four quilts please. And any jelly or jam you can spare." Ma was surprised at having them in our house and how polite they were. She picked out some quilts and jellies, gave it to them, and then stepped back. The tall one said in a deep voice, "Much obliged, ma'am." Then he looked at me and said, "What a strong looking man, isn't he captain?" I almost looked behind me to see who he was talking to. Then I realized he'd just called me a man, which nobody's ever done before.

There was a younger man who said, "Yes sir, Colonel. I'll bet he can ride a horse and shoot a rifle too."

I could feel my heart beating in my throat and said, "You bet I can. I'm a good shot."

Papa stepped in front of me and said, "That's nice of you to say, but he's only a boy."

I stepped around him and was starting to get hot, "No I'm not, I'm almost seventeen!"

Ma said, "No, you just turned sixteen."

The colonel smiled and said, "We have boys his age in our ranks. We fight for freedom just like our grandfathers did. They fought against a king and so are we. Ours is called a president but he acts like a king. You'll hear them say we're fighting for slavery, but it's not true. Less than half of the South owns slaves. We're just fighting for our families and for freedom. Sorry to disturb you and thank you for the goods. Good evening, Ma'am. Good evening, sir. And good evening, sir." That last one was for me.

Course after they left Ma and Papa laid into me. They were red faced and telling me how I shouldn't talk to them like I wanted to join. I didn't say anything but just nodded my head. It didn't matter what they said. That colonel said I was a man. He had fancy braids sewn on his sleeves, bright yellow ones. It was the most beautiful uniform I'd even seen. I swear it was. I don't expect we'll see them again, not with all of the Federals circling around, but I wouldn't mind if they visited again.

At least 'ol Skunky hasn't been around lately. Good riddance.

Jimmy

June 3rd, 1863

Dear Jimmy,

Goodnight, little brother! I swear you'll be the death of me. You need to leave those rebels alone. I don't know who they were or what they were up to but if the wrong Federals would've seen you with them you could get in big trouble. Even if the wrong Federals just heard of you assisting the rebels you could get into trouble. And don't believe what they say. They lie.

Just over a week ago I was on picket duty here at Munfordville. This was some extra picket I volunteered for so Pole wasn't with me. I did it so that I might get an opportunity to catch a rebel spy. I heard a rustling in the woods and at first I thought it sounded like a squirrel, but then my hair bristled. I heard a man's voice groan. He must've stepped in a hole. I wanted to yell out, "Who goes there? Come out or we'll shoot!" But of course all I could get out was, "Stop!" At first it was quiet, but then a soldier came out of the woods with his hands up. I was on picket with a boy name Ben Sowders. As soon as we had some light on his face and ours he said, "Sowders. Gore. Thank goodness it's you! I got lost somehow and couldn't find the campsite."

Ben didn't smile but said flatly, "Sorry Jacobs, but you're not lost. You're a deserter. You'll be coming with us. Green, I'll run and get the sergeant and let the other pickets know. We'll be back in about ten minutes. If he runs, shoot." Ben was never much for a lot of talk, which was why I liked being on picket with him.

If it weren't for roll call I don't know if anyone would have known Jacobs had left. But the sergeant runs through our company and when Jacobs didn't answer and was nowhere to be found three days ago, we all knew he'd quit the army. Sadly, I don't think we missed him. It never felt like he was part of the regiment, more like a visitor that never left.

Once Ben left, Jacobs turned to me and said, "Green Gore! I can't believe my good luck. Look, this will be easy. Just tell them that I ran and your gun jammed and then you missed. Okay? Thanks." He started to head back into the woods when I cocked back my hammer and said, "No! Stop or else!" I stuttered a little, but I was a little shocked by what was going on so I didn't think about it much. Jacobs turned around and walked back towards me.

"What? You're going to turn me in? Look, my wife and children are starving at home. Folks in the area said they'd take care of them and they haven't so I need to go home and tend to my family. Besides, Lincoln made this war about slavery now. That's not why I signed up! I said I'd fight for those against our country, not to free slaves. You understand, don't you?" I shook my head no and kept my gun on him. His smile was gone and in its place was a spark of anger that grew as he spoke.

"Well, I know what you did at Shiloh. You killed Scrap. Your best friend and all you had to do was say something and he'd still be alive. I know your secret and if you turn me in then I'll make sure everyone in camp knows. Pole won't come near you after that, none of the other men will. In fact they may try you for murder. I bet they will, actually. I know you Green. You don't have the stomach to shoot me in the back. So long." He started to turn around and walked into the woods.

What was I to do? Shoot a man in the back or let a deserter go free? I knew I couldn't catch him in the dark once he got away so my only choice was to shoot him in the leg. But there was a part of me that wanted to let him go. He was the only one who saw me at Shiloh with Scrap and I'd love to be rid of him but that would mean I'd have to lie to the colonel and the sergeant and I don't know that I could do that. So I shot him in the back of the leg. He cursed a lot. You'd have thought I killed him, but it really was just a bad scratch. Of course he was going on about how I liked shooting Federals more than rebels and I was really a rebel spy. He was still carrying on when Ben and the sergeant showed up. The sergeant on duty asked for my gun and hit Jacobs in the mouth with the stock. Jacobs looked shocked and was feeling the blood on his lips as the sergeant replied in a calm but threatening tone.

"I don't want to hear another word out of you. Understand? If I hear a peep out of you I'll sew your lips together. And don't think I won't do it." Jacobs minded so I didn't get to see the sergeant sew, although it would've been fine with me.

Jacobs was placed under arrest and was to be tried by the colonel. I thought this was going to be the best answer for me with Jacobs. Caught deserters are sent to prisons up north. Jacobs would be sent away and I wouldn't have to see him anymore. Even though we didn't speak to each other, every time I looked at him I thought of Scrap. Unfortunately for Jacobs, there'd been too many desertions recently because of the

Emancipation Proclamation. The general had given the colonel orders that the next deserter would be executed in front of the company to prevent further desertions. After I heard the news I visited Jacobs. I thought I'd offer to mail a letter for him to his family. At first he wouldn't look at me then he jumped up and said in a quiet but violent voice, "Why do they like you? You can't even speak and you have friends. I've never made friends with anyone in our company even though we've been together for a couple of years. You need to help me escape or I'll tell everyone what you did to Scrap. I swear I will. I've got nothing to lose now."

I'd like to say I didn't even consider helping him out because it was wrong. But all the plans I could think of wouldn't work for one reason or another.

I had three days and three nights to think about what would happen when Jacobs announced how Scrap died. I thought maybe nobody would believe Jacobs. He was a deserter, wasn't he? Then again, I've never known him to be dishonest and it wouldn't be hard to imagine that what he would say made sense. Most of all I worried about how Pole and the sergeant would think of me. Pole is my best pard and even saved my life. Would he still even like me? There's no telling how the sergeant would respond. He could punish me severely or just completely ignore me. Jacobs's last words were the scariest because he was right. He had nothing to lose.

For the execution, all the regiments were ordered to form a square with one side open. At the open side a coffin was placed. Jacobs was marched around the other soldiers to the sound of muffled drums. The sound that means death. The firing line was standing in the middle of the square. They drew straws from each company to see who would be on the firing line. Thank goodness I wasn't on it. Jacobs stopped in front of his coffin and the charge of desertion was read against him. I guess he wanted to see the men who were going to kill him. I could tell he was looking through the ranks until he found me and stopped. He was starting to cry when the colonel asked him if he had anything to say on his own behalf. He looked away from me at the colonel and said, trembling, "Yes. Private John Gore killed Private Andrew Campbell at the Battle of Shiloh. I saw it. He killed him!"

We were still at attention so none of us could move. Besides Scrap's death, it was the worst moment of my life. Even though they couldn't turn their heads I felt hundreds of eyes burning me. The sergeant walked towards me. The colonel said, "Sergeant, this is not the place to—" but the sergeant interrupted.

"Beg your forgiveness sir, but I want to clear this up right now!" He stood within six inches of me and asked in a loud voice, "Private Gore, did you shoot or stab Private Campbell in the Battle of Shiloh? Just shake your head private, I don't have all day." I shook my head side to side. The sergeant turned and said in a loud voice to Jacobs, "You're wrong, John Jacobs. I was there and Private Gore did no such thing. With that knowledge, meet your Maker." A couple of men came and tied a blindfold around his eyes and moved away. A different sergeant gave the order to fire and Jacobs fell back into his coffin. He didn't make much noise. After his coffin was nailed shut he was placed in the hole that he had dug the day before.

That night just as I was ready to go to sleep Pole said my name to see if I was awake. He then said, "I know what Jacobs was talking about. You didn't yell at Scrap to turn around when that rebel came up behind him."

It was like I drank a whole pot of coffee as my mind started racing.

Then Pole said, "It wasn't you that killed Scrap. It was that rebel. It was our first battle. I saw the rebel too and I didn't say anything either. I didn't stutter. I just froze up. I was going to go over to him but you got there first." His voice started cracking at the end and I could see well enough in the moonlight that he was wiping his eyes. His sniffled a bit and then started again.

"I was so ashamed and angry with myself for letting Scrap die that when I saw you on the ground I shot the rebel without asking him to surrender. His gun had to be empty or he would've shot you. I never dreamed I would've done either of those things. But it was my first live battle and I was scared." I didn't say anything. Pole is usually so quiet. Other than when Scrap died, I haven't heard him talk about his feelings. Ever. He paused and took a deep breath in and out before saying, "I can forgive you if you can forgive me." I said I could and we talked a little bit more and then went to sleep. It was the best night's sleep I've had in months.

Putting on a uniform and marching in a battle doesn't make you a man. That rebel colonel is just saying that to get you to join early. Don't listen to him. You are a man. So be a smart one and stay home.

Take care,
Johnny

June 6th, 1863

Dear John,

That was a very sweet letter you wrote. And just so you know John Gore, I don't have a passel of men I write to, just you. And I don't invite every hungry soldier to come to our house for supper, just you. I think you get the idea.

I enjoyed seeing you too and getting to spend time together. I know you don't like to talk around folks, but you're a good storyteller. Course I like hearing about your family and life before the war the most. Your tales make me laugh. And after Winnie, I wasn't sure that would happen again.

We haven't had any more visits from the rebels and I hope that your family hasn't had any either. Ya'll need to stick to the battlefields and leave the rest of us alone. On second thought, you leave the fighting to the rest of the army and maybe you can get a job doing something safe, like being a nurse. I know you want to get promoted but just know I don't care how many threads you have on your sleeve. To me they're just threads.

Of course I want you to come visit again when you can. I'll be looking at the gate until I see you.

I miss you.

Yours truly,
Annie

June 11, 1863

Johnny,

In the end it sounds like getting rid of Jacobs worked out, but it was rough getting there. I think you can put that away and leave it there. Maybe you'll have some good luck in a battle soon.

I'm sorry to tell you bad news. Joshua died. His folks says he got the measles and then pneumonia. He signed up about the same time you did and had written letters to them saying how he liked soldiering. They said he'd done good at Pittsburgh Landing, and was going to move up in the army. Ma baked a pie and we all took it over. Joshua's father talked to Papa about not letting me join up. He kept going on about how the good young boys go and fight for their country but they die on the field because their general wasn't as smart as the southern ones, or they die around camp from something that didn't have anything to do with fighting. He was proud his son went and died for the country but as he was crying, he said, "I didn't send my boy off to die for a bunch of slaves." He didn't say much after that. Ma and Papa just looked at me and we left a little while later. I didn't say anything riding home and Papa just said a few words. Good for us that Ma was there and she talked and talked. She didn't say nothing about the war or Joshua or me signing up. She knew if we started talking about the war Papa may get upset. It never occurred to anyone that a soldier could die from measles. What a waste. I know this will be hard for you to hear as ya'll were close.

Jimmy

G | **13** | **Ky.**

John J. Co. Moore

Pvt., Co. A, 13 Reg't Kentucky Infantry.

Appears on

Company Muster Roll

for May & June, 1863.

Present or absent _Present_

Stoppage, $ 100 for

Due Gov't, $ 100 for

Remarks:

Book mark:

Casterling

(858) *Copyist.*

CHAPTER EIGHT

July 1ˢᵗ, 1863

Dear Annie,

I lost count how many times I read your last letter. I just wish it were longer. I miss you. It hadn't been that long but it feels like years since I was at your house. We're being sent to check on railroads around middle Kentucky. We're mostly in Munfordville but we'll be anywhere within a hundred miles of here for a few days. I keep volunteering for Campbellsville but the sergeant keeps saying no.

There was a boy from a different regiment that was walking by the other day that I could've sworn was Joshua Burk. He looked just like him, down to the freckles. Joshua and I grew up going to the same church, but he joined a different Kentucky regiment to be with his kin. I'll never forget before I left for camp when Joshua and I went fishing. It was cold, but we had good luck. We caught half a sack of fish and couldn't wait to get home. We talked the whole way back and then just as we were almost at his house, he had a funny look on his face. He said the sack was a little light. He checked and sure enough, there was a hole in the sack and no fish. We saw the hole at the same time and looked at each other and then started laughing.

We must've laughed for ten minutes, stumbling over each other, thinking how we were going to explain it. I just found out from Jimmy that Joshua died. He didn't die while charging up a hill or defending a fort. He died from measles and pneumonia. It's hard to understand why he's gone.

I try to remember a verse that I read the other day that helps. 1 Corinthians 10:13, "There hath no temptation taken you but such as is common to man: but God is faithful, who will not suffer you to be tempted above that ye are able; but will with the temptation also make a way to escape, that ye may be able to bear it." There's been times when I've wondered if God has me confused with someone else who can stand more than me.

There's a particular Federal sergeant who's been going to my house and been ugly to Jimmy and my folks. I've been trying to find him but haven't had any luck. He can't hide forever. Even if I do find him I'll just be able to tell my sergeant on him and hope he does something. We'll see.

Take care,
John

July 3rd, 1863

Dear Jimmy,

Hearing about Joshua was tough. I remember one time his pa had planted some potatoes and they'd been busy with his ma being sick so they hadn't weeded that part of the garden well. I was over there helping and another older man came over to dig some of the potatoes. Problem was there were so many weeds he couldn't find them. He came over to Joshua's pa and said, "Mr. Burk, I think the only man who can find those taters is the man who planted those taters." Joshua and I signed up about a month later.

I've been meaning to talk to you about slavery. We've had an escaped slave come to our camp and he hitched himself to Pole and me, so we've gotten to know him really well. I'll just say that he's not a horse or a mule to be traded and treated like one. He's a man. I know you feel like what happens to them doesn't concern you. I felt the same way when I joined. Maybe the rebels are right about having their own rights, maybe they're right about being able to form their own country. To be honest there's a part of me that wants to let them go and say good riddance. There's been so much loss from this war that I'm ready for it to be over. But now I know slavery is wrong. You've never seen the scars on a young slave's back from being whipped. It's awful. The whole business is rotten and has to end. I wouldn't have given it two shakes when I signed up, but now I'd be willing to die if it meant an end to slavery. It's that bad. Trust me.

Take care,
Johnny

July 10th, 1863

Dear John,

I'm so sorry to hear about the passing of your friend. We've had too many men from around here die. Some have been from bullets but most have been from sickness like Joshua. There's no making sense of the war. I'm still dealing with losing Winnie. I thought I was over it but last week Ma was down in her back again lying on the bed. She wasn't trying to be mean but I heard her say something like, "I sure wish Winnie was here to help." And I pounced like a cat. Lord help me I don't know what came over me but I went straight to her bed and talked to her like I never dared talked to her or Pa before. I had everything out of my mouth before I even knew what I'd said.

"Well it was all your fault! If you and your so-called back pain wouldn't have acted up then I would've been out there in time to save her. It's your fault Winnie's dead!"

As soon as I said it I put both hands over my mouth like the words came out on their own. When I said it I was angry, but then I felt ashamed that I'd spoken to Ma that way. And then she started crying saying, "I know. I'm sorry." Then I started crying and telling her it wasn't her fault. We were both crying and I was kneeling down and was holding her when I heard Pa coming in the house. He opened the door and saw us there crying and stood there for a good five seconds and then looked around the inside of the house like he'd never seen it before. He started to speak, held his hand up and then turned around and headed back out. We looked at each other and laughed.

We both said we were sorry and that we missed Winnie very much. I've always been closer to Pa than her. It was the first time in my life to really feel close to her. I can't believe it took Winnie's death to bring us together, but we've been talking a lot recently and I've loved it.

I'll share with you a verse that has helped me. Romans 15:13, "Now the God of hope fill you with all joy and peace in believing, that ye may abound in hope, through the power of the Holy Ghost."

I pray that you don't lose hope. I miss you.

Yours truly,
Annie

July 18ᵗʰ, 1863

Dear Annie,

Thank you for the letter, including the verse. If there's something I need right now, it's hope. The only thing worse than being angry is being angry and helpless to do anything about it.

So you remember me telling you about Isaac? He's a runaway slave that's been hanging around Pole and me. He's about my age, I think. He doesn't exactly know his birthday. We've been getting used to Isaac and like having him around. We're not the only men that have former slaves in camp—called "contraband" although we treat Isaac better than the others are treated. As Isaac has gotten to know us, he trusts us. At first he wouldn't say much against his former master. I guess he was so used to not saying anything negative in case it ever got back to him. But now he'll answer any question we ask right away. It had never occurred to me to think what it was like living as a slave. I'd seen his scars from being whipped by his overseer. He'd get one lash a year for when they said his birthday was to remind him what would happen if he tried to escape. His birthday was March 1st, which was when every male on his farm's birthday was. He told of seeing young children, just a few years old, chained together and without a stich of clothing being paraded through the farm as they were going off to be sold. They would take the children when the women were all working out in the field or in the house so they wouldn't notice. One time a young woman noticed when they were taking the babies and she ran screaming. The overseer came back and punched her in the face to warn the others. From the stories Isaac told, that overseer was the meanest man I'd ever heard of. Mr. Wilcox is his name. Thank goodness the Emancipation Proclamation put an end to slavery.

One day last week there was a man at the gate wearing a white suit and hat. It's so hot here you'll sweat sitting in the shade, so his brow was dripping and he had a handkerchief in both hands to wipe off the shower. He had a round, red face and a large belly. We all just figured he was a sutler asking if he could sell us RG (that stands for rotgut, which is the awfulest type of whiskey they make). I don't know why but when he was directed towards our sergeant I got interested in him. I could see them talking and then the sergeant walked with him to the colonel's tent. I went and got Pole and asked where Isaac was. Pole said Isaac had gone to the sutler's to buy spices. It seemed like I turned around and then came the man in the white suit, the sergeant, and the colonel. There was another man behind the man in the white suite, a thick-chested man carrying chains in his hands. The colonel called Pole and I to attention an introduced the man in the white suit as Mr. Wilcox.

With those few words that fat, sweaty man in the suit turned into a monster in my eyes. The colonel was talking but all I could think about was all the evil that man had done. Those big hands and chubby fingers had held the whip that had whipped Isaac, given him all of those scars on his back. I came to while standing when I heard Pole ask the colonel question, "But didn't Lincoln free the slaves?"

The colonel pursed his lips, blinked his eyes several times, and said in a low but firm voice, "He did, but only in states in rebellion against the Union. Kentucky is not officially part of the rebellion, so slavery is not illegal here. I'm afraid the young man staying with you will need to go with Mr. Wilcox."

It was like I had been in a deep sleep and was slowly waking up. I was starting to understand what was happening and wanted to scream at the colonel and the sergeant for letting that pig come and drag Isaac away. Just as I was coming to my senses I could see Isaac walking up behind us.

He was looking down as he was walking up to our tent and wasn't paying attention to anyone. He put the spices in our tent and turned around and saw us with the colonel, the sergeant, and Wilcox. When Isaac saw Mr. Wilcox it was like he was seeing the devil himself. Pole and I stared at Isaac, waiting to see how he'd respond. Isaac dove at our feet and grabbed our ankles. I could feel him trembling as he was starting the cry, "I ain't goin back! I can't!"

Since Isaac was around our legs, Mr. Wilcox looked at the colonel and said, "That boy's my property and I want him now!" The colonel looked at us and nodded. Mr. Wilcox smiled, never taking his eyes off of Isaac. He raised his eyebrows as he said, "Chains." With that the muscular man behind him walked around with a large clasp to put around Isaac's neck. Isaac was lying face down on the ground, shaking as the man opened up the gray chains sprinkled with rust. Just as the clasp was on his neck Isaac turned around and screamed, "NO! You ain't puttin that on me!"

Mr. Wilcox's smile turned into a snarl, "Oh you're goin to wear that chain, boy. And you're goin to pay." Then that awful, sweaty pig took out a whip and started lashing the poor boy. All Isaac could do was put his hands over his head, but the lashes on his ribs would make him pull his arms down.

After the first couple of lashes drew bright red blood I started to speak. I was trying to say, "Stop!" But I was angry and all that came out was some hissing. All I could think of was stopping Mr. Wilcox. I started towards my tent to get my rifle. Still looking straight ahead, Pole's arm went across my chest to hold me back. He never looked at me, but shook his head side to side a couple of times. He knew what I was thinking and wanted to do the same, but knew better. I wanted to take that whip and cut that evil man to pieces, but I had to stand there and watch.

We stood and did nothing as poor Isaac screamed and jerked with each strike. The lashes were getting harder as Mr. Wilcox was turning into a wild animal, cursing the poor boy. After a dozen lashes and screams, the colonel said, "That's enough Mr. Wilcox, take your property and leave." Mr. Wilcox was breathing heavy now. He held up the whip and looked at the colonel. The colonel raised his voice just a little and sternly ordered, "Now." Mr. Wilcox realized where he was and who the colonel was. At that the other man placed the clasp around Isaac's neck and placed two more clasps around his hands with chains connecting them. Isaac had been twisting on the ground with the whipping and he was now facing me. His eyes had been closed as he lay there crying, but he opened them and our eyes met.

He didn't resist the chains. As Isaac stared at me, his eyes asked, "Why?" I felt a heavy weight on me like I'd marched a thousand miles. I could barely stand up my legs felt so weak. Isaac thought he'd found freedom, but it was a lie. He never made another sound, but tears kept streaming down his cheeks. Finally, I couldn't take it anymore and had to look down as he was dragged away. Pole said nothing could be done. It was the law.

I haven't seen Isaac again or Mr. Wilcox. Someone who had picket south of here said he saw a young slave hanging from a tree. The slave had been whipped so badly and had been dead for several days so he couldn't make out if it was Isaac or not. Pole and I never talked about him again.

Before the war I didn't care any more about the slaves than I did for mules. They didn't bother me and I didn't bother them. There's been a lot of men who've left our army because they didn't sign up to fight against slavery and Lincoln has turned the war into that. I understand that a lot of rebels just feel they're fighting for their farms and their freedom to live the way they feel is right. And if I was in the South I'd probably have signed up to fight too. But slavery is wrong. I'd never seen it up close before against someone I knew. I don't care what any rebel says or what some bad Federal soldiers do. Slavery has to got to go and that's that.

I think we're going to be on the move soon and I'll be glad when we do. I want to leave this place.

Take care,
John

July 30, 1863

Dear John,

I'm so sorry you had such a time with that slave's owner. I have to admit that I felt along the same lines as you did when you joined. We never owned slaves and none of our people have as far as I know. There's other people in the county that do, but they're rich. Since I've never been around slaves much I never gave any thought to how they were treated. I believe what you say, but I can't believe that people would act like that. I've never really been for slavery, so reading your story made me against it. My folks are not as likely to change, but they hate the rebels so much that anything that goes against the rebels they'll like.

I've gotten along better with Ma recently. She's finally stopped wearing black, which is good for everyone. When she's wearing that all of the time it makes the whole house gloomy. She has trouble cooking because her back hurts her so much. She can stand if she's leaning over something but if she tries to stand straight she says the pain is something awful. There's nothing that we can see and she hasn't hurt her back any recently, so it's hard for Pa and I to understand how her back is hurting her so much. Sometimes she'll cry out at night that her foot is on fire, but of course she's been in bed the whole time.

I wish you could visit again so we could be together. I love reading your letters, even if the last one wasn't too jolly.

Stay safe,
    Annie

August 8th, 1863
Pomeroy, Ohio

Dear Jimmy,

I haven't heard back from you, but maybe you're just busy. I want to tell you about chasing Morgan, but I'll need to go back to the latter part of July when several regiments were set on catching him, including ours. We finally left Munfordville and followed Morgan north. We slept a little, ate a little, and marched a lot. We smelled like a pack of hogs. We teamed up with General Shackelford and Colonel Rue. We had a fight with some of Morgan's men and captured a small herd of rebels, but Morgan got away. Our regiment helped to guard some of the prisoners while others kept up after Morgan. We were closing in and Morgan knew it, but even with the end near he had a few cards to play.

Sometime before, and I don't know when or where, Morgan had captured a Union officer named Burbick. He was saving him in case we got too close. And we did. So Morgan surrendered to his own prisoner, Burbick, and then sent him back to Shackelford. It sounds silly, but Morgan was hoping it would be confusing and give the rebels time to get away. But Colonel Rue caught up with Morgan before Burbick returned. Clever to the end, Morgan bluffed and tried to get Rue to surrender to him, claiming his division was bigger. Rue saw through the trick and just smiled. Morgan was sent to prison.

We had a skirmish the other day and I wish a writer for the newspaper had been there. We saw a rebel company of scouts in a clearing, just waiting on the day.

From the clearing there was a narrow path through some woods. Our captain positioned us in the trees on one side of the path but we were extra quiet and entered through the woods so the rebels wouldn't see us. Once we were in position, another Union company acted as bait to pull them up. The rebels were so focused on chasing our other company that they followed them into the narrow piece. Their pumpkin rind was following behind and just as he spotted us and gave the order for his troops to turn and fire on us, our captain's bugle sounded. The bugle was the signal for us to let them have it. And we did. It was like collecting the chickens with the henhouse door closed. We took them by surprise and peddled a lot of lead. The war fog was so thick you couldn't see what you were shooting at, but we kept at it. Sometimes when you're on the winning side, especially when you're not taking too many casualties, battles aren't so bad. And like I told you before, fighting will wear you out more than anything else you can do. Even a short fight for about thirty minutes will use you up for a whole day.

I always hated going to sleep when it's this hot. I'd just lie there and sweat all night feeling awful, but not now. After a day of hard marching or if we have a fight, I can go right to sleep. I haven't slept on a feather bed since I left home, but even with sleeping on the ground, I've had my best nights' sleep under the stars out in an open field. I would've never believed it, but it's true.

By the way, I'm sending a package with a couple of wrapped gifts for you and Ma, but you can't open them till Christmas! I never know when we're going to have to leave this area so I went ahead and sent them now.

I was able to get permission for a couple of days in Campbellsville so that I could see Annie. We were both so glad to see each other. But after Winnie, they've changed. When I was getting ready to go back to my camp, her Pa took hold of my shoulders, looked me in the eye, and said, "You get those rebels, you hear. And don't hold nothing back!" His eyes were starting to water so he turned away and walked outside. She's the one for me. I've only got one more year in Abe's army and then Annie and I'll be able to get hitched and start a family. Just one more year.

Take care,
Johnny

August 10th, 1863

Dear Annie,

We caught Morgan! You'll be happy to know that his head was shaved and he was paraded around Cincinnati as a prisoner of war. He's in prison there and can rot for all I care. We got him.

I hope your Ma's back feels better. I'm sure when she's down it means more chores for you. I heard someone say one time that if you place a knife under your bed it will help your back. My Pa did that one time and it took two weeks. I don't know if it works but she could try it when she has a bad spell.

When I joined all I could think about was getting promoted. I wanted to do something really brave so I could be promoted and folks around town would know it. I kept wanting to impress the sergeant. It was pretty much all I thought about to keep me going. Whenever I was marching for a long time or had to get up early or pull a wagon through the mud, I kept thinking about stripes on my sleeve, anything was better than private.

A few days ago I was standing behind a tent when I heard someone pretend they were stuttering. I could tell they were mocking me. There were a few of them there as I could hear them laughing. Then I heard the sergeant come by and tell them to stop. He said I was a good soldier. That he wished he had several more of me. I couldn't believe what I was hearing. It was the best thing anybody has said about me before. Ever. Then one of them asked the sergeant if I would get promoted. The sergeant replied, "Corporal? No. What if he had to give commands in battle when seconds mean life or death? Treat him fair. This is my warning to you. Good evening."

I was grateful for him standing up for me, but he burned up my dreams like a match to paper. I'm not going to lie, it hurts a lot. I'm having to face that my life can't be built on getting promoted. That's why your letters mean a lot to me. You give me something to look forward to.

I'm a little surprised I haven't heard back from Jimmy recently. Maybe he's busy with working on the farm or perhaps he didn't like may last letter about how I thought slavery was wrong. Jimmy's not mean. He's just short-tempered and doesn't always think through what he does. I'm sure he's fine.

We're back in Kentucky, headed down to Munford-ville again. I don't know how long we'll be here now that Morgan's won't be causing any more trouble.

Take care,
John

August 12th, 1863

Dear Johnny,

This isn't a letter I want to write, but I have to. Ol' Skunky came by here again a couple of days ago. He didn't have that officer with him this time but he did have a covey of soldiers. He came up smiling with his ugly beard and nasty smell. It was in the evening as the sky was turning blue to red. We were all outside in the garden. Ma saw them first and let out a "Oh for heaven's sake" as me and Papa looked up. Skunky came right over to me and didn't even look at Ma or Papa.

"So boy, there's no officer here today. Are you going to give me a chance to straighten you out? You just give me a reason. That's all I need." I was trying not to get excited. He spit down on my right shoe. He just chewed and looked me in the eye. At first I was looking right back but then I remembered that I didn't want to get Ma upset so I looked down. When I did he laughed a little and turned to go into our house. Ma followed at a distance and then he came out with some jellies and a quilt that was Grandma Gore's.

Ma went up and begged him not to take it, "I'll get you another one that's a lot warmer. That's a family quilt."

He ignored her. She pressed closer and he spat back, "I'll take what I want. If I want to put this on my horse there ain't nothing you're gonna do about it." He looked at me and then quickly looked back at her, his big hand pressed on her chest, knocking her down on the porch. "Go back to your kitchen where you belong."

Papa and I rushed to help her up. I didn't know how she'd react but I could tell by her eyes that she was mad as a hornet. She didn't say a word. She didn't have to. Skunky took our calf that we'd been feeding out. The men with him laughed whenever he did anything and cheered him on. They left and we went in to eat. I don't think we spoke for a hour and then finally Ma said, "Lord I hope this war is over soon. I want the Federals to win, but I'd hold the coat for the man that could knock some sense into that sergeant." Papa was quiet and I felt like he was watching me. After dinner they talked about how sad it was that we're getting punished by our own soldiers. It's causing many Kentucky folks to favor the rebels, even though they're losing. Ma has kept talking under her breath how she wants Skunky to get his.

This is hard for me to write but I don't have a choice. I'm going to join the rebel army. I know you'll be upset with me. Ma and Papa will too. Maybe folks in the South have a right to own slaves, I don't know. Maybe their states should have a right to do what they please without Lincoln telling them what to do, I don't know. But I do know I saw a Federal soldier knock down Ma. I shouldn't have to take that and I'm not meaning too. I don't know who I'm going to join or how, but it's going to be soon. Don't bother writing a letter to Ma to keep me from joining. I'll be gone soon after this is mailed.

I never thought I'd say I didn't want to see you but I hope I don't see you for the next year or two. I know once I join that we're on different sides and I'll be expected to fight to the death and kill any Federal soldier in front of me. If we meet on a battlefield, I won't fight. I'm not joining to fight against you or Lincoln. I'm willing to die just for the chance to find Skunky. And I won't stop. You may say I've lost my sense to join the rebels but you didn't see him push Ma down. If there weren't a war on and some man did that, you'd fight him to the death. I know you would. Well, I'm not going to let the war be an excuse to let some outlaw get away with it just because he wears a uniform. I'll wear a different uniform and then it'll be legal.

Sorry.

Jimmy

| _A_ | **13** | **Ky.** |

John J. C. Gore

Pvt. ..., Co. A, 13 Reg't Kentucky Infantry.

Appears on

Company Muster Roll

for _July & Aug_ , 186_3_.

Present or absent _Present_

Stoppage, $ _100_ for _____

Due Gov't, $ _100_ for _____

Remarks: _____

Book mark: _____

Easterling

(858)   *Copyist.*

CHAPTER NINE

September 2, 1863

Dear Annie,

I just received about the worst news I can think of. Jimmy's joined the rebels. I still can't believe it. I knew he was angry about the Federal soldiers acting ugly and stealing from us. That same lousy sergeant came around again and this time he knocked Ma down in front of Papa and Jimmy. There was nothing Jimmy or Papa could do and that was too much for Jimmy. He left to find a rebel outfit to join. The young fool has no idea what he's about to do. He still thinks this is some game he would play at school. I'm so mad at him right now I could beat him till it hurt him to breathe. But I'm scared for him, too. I've seen so many awful sights since joining up and I don't want him to know how evil war can be. I've told him about fighting and battles but I left a lot out. A lot that I wish I could forget but fear I never will.

Jimmy's never seen the rebels attack close to home. I told him what they did to you. And he's never seen slavery, not the evil I've seen. All he knows is this one Federal sergeant was mean and got the best of him. Jimmy couldn't stand knowing he lost so he had to join to get revenge. Except Jimmy doesn't like to just get even, he wants to win. It doesn't help that so many folks from Kentucky are siding with the rebels. He won't be seen as a traitor around home.

How I wish I could find that sergeant that turned my little brother against our country. It's his fault. Pole's told me there isn't anything I could do even if I did find him. He's a sergeant and I'm a private. If I attacked him he'd have me killed. But at least I could prove to him I'm a Federal soldier. That would help. If he knew I was fighting alongside him then surely he wouldn't go and knock down my mother and steal from my family. He is a sergeant after all and has to have some measure of character.

We haven't left Munfordville recently. I've heard we might start pushing south to bring an end to the war. Lord I'm ready for the war to be over, especially before Jimmy gets himself hurt.

Take care,
John

September 12, 1863

Dear John,

That was so sad to hear about Jimmy. I hardly know what to say. Course there's a good chance the war might end soon before either of you get hurt. And even though I'm sure you'd like to tan his hide for the worry, I think you'll forgive him. At least he has a chance to come home.

I hope you're right about that sergeant. That he's not as mean as those rebels that came around here. I had no idea just how awful some people could be. It's not fair he can treat you that way because he has extra thread on his sleeves. At times it seems life is more unfair than fair.

We've been busy harvesting and canning. The sad part is that when I'm working I don't know who's going to be eating it. There's no telling if a group of soldiers from either side may come in and take our food if they take a notion to.

I have to admit that at times like this I get low. I start to wonder why God is allowing all of this to happen. Do you ever feel that way? I remind myself of Proverbs 3: 5-6, "Trust in the Lord with all thine heart and lean not unto your own understanding. In all thine ways acknowledge him and he will direct thy paths."

Last week Cricket was out making her usual rounds and ran into a skunk. I don't know if she got the skunk or not, but the skunk sure got her. Papa and I were in the garden when we heard Ma yelling at her, "Lord have mercy, dog. What have you gotten yourself into?

Don't you bring your nasty hide over here! You better go down to the creek and get yourself a bath!"

Poor Cricket drooped down. She knew she was in trouble. And boy did she stink. I went down to the creek with her and threw a stick in there a few times to wash her a little, but it didn't do much good. I tried to wash her with some soap, but I think the stink just has to wear off. I told her she couldn't sleep on our porch and that she'd have to stay by the oak in the front and I'd throw her some scraps. Ma's told her that if she catches her on her porch while he smelled like that Papa would have a new hat. I never thought of Cricket as being a really smart dog, but she seems to know everything we said. I suppose the next time she sees a skunk she'll turn around and go the other way.

Again, I'm sorry for your sad news. But keep hope.

Annie

September 22, 1863

Dear Annie,

Thank you for the letter and the verse. I've been clinging to hope ever since Scrap died, but especially over the last few weeks. I feel badly complaining to you about only possibly losing a brother. I don't even know how much help he'll be to the other side. He can't shoot that well and when he walks through the woods it's like a hog dragging a chain. But he's my brother and I love him. I've never told him that. I always felt I didn't have to say it because it was understood. Now I'd give anything to be able to talk with him again. I'd hug him and tell him how happy I was that he was alive. Then I'd kill him while I was yelling at him for scaring myself and my folks to death. I'm the closest to him and have always tried my best to help him out. With him leaving I feel like I failed him. Perhaps if I'd have gone home I could have talked to him directly and it would have made a difference. Maybe I didn't try hard enough to find that no-good sergeant. Or I didn't say the right things in my last letter to him. I don't know.

We've marched enough over the last month to do me till spring. General Burnside took command of our regiment and had us join the 23rd Corps of the Army of the Ohio with General Hartsuf. Hartsuf had us march through Kentucky and all the way into East Tennessee. We walked up and down hollers and hills, sometimes covering thirty miles a day. My legs and feet were so sore. I felt like somebody'd beat me with a tobacco stick. And I mean somebody big. When you're marching that far, every pound seems to be an anvil weighing you down. Some men in other regiments did throw away their heavy coats and blankets, but if anyone in our regiment did that, the sergeant made him pick it up. He's not big on waste.

Just yesterday, under the command of General Burnside, we took control of the Cumberland Gap, which is the key to East Tennessee. The Gap is the easiest way to travel through the Cumberland Mountains. I'm told one of the first to come through here was Daniel Boone. Anyway, General Burnside was able to trick Confederate General Frazier into surrendering, even though Frazier had more men and had a good defensive position. Burnside had three different brigades surround Frazier and made him think we were a lot stronger than we were. I guess Frazier didn't want to fight in a battle he knew he was going to lose, so the rebels laid down their guns and gave us their batteries. It was the cleanest battle I'd ever heard of and now we have Knoxville and the Cumberland Gap. While some of the brigades went to Knoxville to strengthen the forts there, we went down the road a piece near a town called Loudon. This is where we expect the rebels to cross the Tennessee River when they're coming to take back Knoxville. We know they're going to return, we just don't know when. So we're here to slow them down.

It looks like we may be here in Tennessee for a spell, but I don't know how long. I expect to be back home directly.

Thank you for your letter and encouragement.

Take care,
    John

October 2, 1863

Dear John,

I hope your shoes still have a sole on them. I heard some soldiers had walked so much their toes were sticking out. I just hope you don't get a little rock in your shoe. All it takes is one small pebble and after a spell it will seem like that's all you can think about. I like reading about you being in battles where nobody shoots. I pray that's the only type you'll be in from now on. Maybe the rebels will figure out they're not going to win and just quit.

I've been thinking about us a lot. It helps me to think about something happy and not about the war. We don't ever speak about Winnie because it's still too hard when she comes up. I used to forget and would start a story, "You remember the time when Winnie …" But it didn't take long to see that neither of my folks wanted to talk about her. It's still too raw.

I like it when you have some of your hair sticking up at the crown. I'm not making fun so don't get upset. I think it looks cute. You're normally really quiet but then occasionally you'll get excited about something when you're talking and your voice gets loud. Ma told me she looked out on the porch a time or two when we were talking cause she didn't figure you could talk like that. It was when you were talking about yourself, Scrap, and Pole seeing who could swim across the river when the ice was along the bank. I also like when you held my hand when you said goodbye. Your hands are strong and rough from doing hard work.

I miss you.

Love,
    Annie

P.S. I hate mushy green beans. Ma just keeps boiling them and boiling them till there ain't much flavor. Course I eat them and don't say anything but I don't like them. This really isn't important, it's just something I wanted to share since we had green beans tonight.

October 14th, 1863
Loudon, TN

Dear Annie,

Thank you for your letter. I don't especially like green beans either but I can handle them better than beef liver. Fortunately we don't eat it much, but Lord that smell is enough to turn my stomach. That's a night when I don't eat any lean so I don't have to eat the fat. I don't know how it is at your house but if we want to eat the lean meat we have to eat the fat too. I usually just put the fat in a biscuit and swallow it whole. But on liver nights I pass.

From the first time I saw you, looking up from the floor after falling, I loved your smile. Not just the smile when you're happy or when you're trying to be nice, but the smile when you're laughing so hard you're crying. Your eyes squint together and you don't laugh loud at first but then you start to make a sound after about ten seconds. I swear I'd fall off your porch a hundred times if I thought it would make you smile like that. I've thought about that smile so many times when I've been in a rough patch and it helps.

I also like the sound of your voice. I know you think it's too high and sounds like a little girl, but I wouldn't change it for anything. Sometimes it's harder for me to remember it exactly, but I'd know it within a word or two if I heard it. I've been trying to think of something to share with you about me, something that nobody else knows and I've never talked about before.

I hate the letters *B*, *D*, and *G*. These are the worst for my stuttering. It's not as bad when the letters are in the middle of the word compared to when they start it. Sometimes I also struggle with S and W, which makes it the devil to ask a question. My curse is my last name. Sometimes when I'm asked to state my name it makes me nervous, which makes my stuttering worse. I've even thought about making up a different last name, like Morris. I could say it fine and for most people it wouldn't matter, although in the army it would. When I'm talking with someone who asks me a question, I have to think out all of my words to make sure they don't start with one of these letters. If they do then I have to think of something else to say, which can make talking very tiring for me. I'm not saying this because I don't like talking with you or I'm complaining. I love talking with you. But when I'm with others then I'm not going to speak much because it's so much harder for me. Folks that don't stutter don't think about it.

I still haven't heard from Jimmy or from my folks. I don't think they want to tell me because they're afraid I'll worry. They're right. I wish I could go and take his place and let him go home. It'd be worth it to me to fight for the rebels as long as he could go home safe. I know that doesn't make sense, but it would for me.

Okay, so let me try another poem.

> When you are far and no one near
> Think of one that loves you so dear.

Take care,
John

October 24ᵗʰ, 1863

Dear John,

That was a very sweet letter. I like to look into your green eyes. Everyone in my family has brown eyes. Your eyes are kind and happy when we're together on the porch but also sad when you're talking with my folks. I'm sorry it's harder for you to talk. I can't imagine having to think out everything I said, although Pa would say I'd be a lot better off if I didn't just say whatever came into my head.

After those rebels came to our farm, the house doesn't look and feel the same. It's like an old friend you thought you knew, but who was wearing a mask the whole time. Sometimes I look at our house and it feels like it's somebody else's. I don't want to live here any longer than I have to. I want to move to a house that will feel like a home again. When you're here with me, it feels like home.

I liked your poem. Here's one for you.

> When far away and out of sight
> Three little words to you I will write.
> I love you.

Annie

October 29, 1863

Johnny,

I'm back home. I'm sure you're sore about me leaving and I don't blame you. It wasn't one of my smarter moves, but you don't know what it was like seeing Ma struck down. I had to do something. Feeling like there was nothing I could do was like an anvil sitting on my chest. Anyways, I'm home and managed to not get myself shot. If you write back I'll tell you what happened.

Ma and Papa cried when I came back. I thought Papa would beat me with the buggy whip and Ma would give me the awfulest tongue lashing of my life. I didn't even know for sure if they'd take me back or if they'd make me sleep in the barn for a while. But they didn't. They cried and then I cried and tried to say I'm sorry through the snot.

So I'm saying I'm sorry to you, too. You were probably worried about what trouble I'd get myself into. I won't do it again. Unless they come to make me fight, I'm done with it. And if Skunky comes back and wants to take a pig then I'll let him take a pig. I'll even pick one out for him. I won't like it and I'll hope he falls and gets manure all over himself but I won't push him.

I'll mind from now on. I promise.

Jimmy

| | 13 | Ky. |

John J. C. Gore

Prvt., Co. A, 13 Reg't Kentucky Infantry.

Appears on

Company Muster Roll

for *Sept. & Oct.*, 186 *3*.

Present or absent *Present.*

Stoppage, $ 100 for

Due Gov't, $ 100 for

Remarks:

Book mark:

Enlisting

(358)   *Copyist.*

CHAPTER TEN

November 6th, 1863
Knoxville, TN

Dear Jimmy,

You're right I'm sore. Papa may not of beat you with a buggy whip, but I would have. Hard. I started to write you a letter about a dozen times. I was going to tell you off for putting Ma, Papa, and me through this. But I've cooled off some. I'm still mad but I'm glad you're home safe. That's what matters. I hope you finally have some sense of what joining the army is like.

We took Knoxville but there wasn't any fight. The rebels are close but they're not attacking us yet.

I'd like to hear what happened.

John

November 7th, 1863

Dear Annie,

I heard from Jimmy. I don't know the details yet, but he quit the rebels and came back home. Ornery mule. He's lucky I wasn't there when he came back. I would've let him have it. Anyway, it felt like I was packing an extra fifty pounds and now it's off. Thank you for your prayers.

You'll be glad to know that even though we're only a stone's throw from the rebels, except for a couple of little arguments here and there, there hasn't been any real shooting. But we're looking for a fight here directly. The rebs are likely to come back to take Knoxville. Whenever someone asks our sergeant about the rebels he always says, "Let 'em come and see what the 13th has for 'em." I'm fond of the sergeant now. I can remember hating him, thinking that nobody could actually love a man so cruel. But now I see him as a father that believes in discipline. Sometimes it still seems that he enjoyed the punishments more than he should have, but in the end he knew that the discipline would keep us alive. I think he likes me, too. He doesn't show much emotion, even when he's angry. Still, the way he's made comments here and there leads me to think he likes me as much as anyone.

> Remember me early, remember me late.
> Remember the kiss at the garden gate.

I know we haven't kissed yet, but a boy can hope.

Love,
John

November 14, 1863

Johnny,

So I wrote you that letter before I left and I also wrote one to Ma and Papa. I felt I had to tell them why I was running off, that I couldn't take it anymore. I never wanted to fight against you. But I had to go.

So I set out with Red and made it as far as Cub Run when I came up on a couple of men that looked like soldiers. I came up behind them and said, "How ya'll doing? Are you with the South?" Both of them turned around and quicker than a cat's paw had their guns on me and cocked. They were dirty with brown smudges on their face. Their beards looked like they'd been left to field. I put up my hands and said, "Wait, don't shoot! I'm looking to join up." They both squinted their eyes under their floppy hats and looked at each other.

"Who you think we're with, boy?"

"I don't know, sir. Since you're not in a Federal uniform I expect you'd be with the rebels. Look, there's been some Federals coming around our farm and stealing from us. Last week one of them pushed down my Ma. I couldn't fight him there because he had a company with him, but I figured I could join up and then we could go get him." The one on the right smiled while the one on the left looked puzzled.

"Anybody followin you, boy?"

"No sir, not that I know of."

"What's your name boy?" Now I guess at the time I didn't trust them anymore than they trusted me.

"Bobby. Bobby Keebler. Sir. From around Hardyville. Sir."

As we were talking they were moving closer to me. I was starting to smell them as well. They didn't smell much better than Skunky, maybe worse, like meat gone bad. After they had a look at me up close they pulled away and talked between themselves so I couldn't hear. At first they were arguing back and forth in a loud whisper. I was trying to hear but not act like I was trying to hear. It didn't work. Every so often they'd stop talking and look over at me. Then they'd start arguing again. It seemed like I waited fifteen minutes before they came back to talk with me. The one on the right nodded his head and spoke.

"Okay, Bobby Keebler from around Hardyville. I'm Levi and this is Reuben. We're rebels alright, although we're with a special outfit. Our colonel is Champ Ferguson. Our duty is to go around and cause trouble for the Federals in these parts. Blowin up bridges, tearin up tracks, and lettin the locals know we're around. If you're up to joinin us then come along. If not, then I'll give you ten seconds to turn around and get out of here alive." Reuben looked at him like he wasn't so sure about me and Reuben just nodded his head. Well, this was why I'd left so I figured I'd go with them.

They rode on either side of me and kept asking me about what kind of food I had and how much powder and bullets I had with me. I felt like they were sizing me up, like a hog before slaughter. They asked about my family and I told them everything I knew about

Bobby's family, including that his brother was fighting for the Federals.

I thought they'd be mad, but Levi said, "That's okay, I have kin fighting for them too. But if we're on the field I'd shoot them. I wouldn't give it anymore thought then shooting a squirrel."

Reuben spoke again. "What about the pickets?"

Levi smiled again and said, "Yea, that's a good idea. We'll let Bobby see a little action."

We started heading to Munfordville and about five miles out they got off of their horses and told me to do the same. We tied them to a tree and walked about fifty yards through some thick brush and then Levi put his finger to his lips to tell me to be quiet. Then he opened a view through some briars and I could see about twenty yards away two men standing and talking to each other. They were Federals. Both Levi and Reuben took aim and very softly Levi said, "Ready, aim, fire." Both of the soldiers dropped although it didn't look like either was dead. At the time I didn't remember where you were, but I knew you'd been taking some extra picket duty. I told Levi I needed to see if one of them was my brother.

"Not unless you want us to shoot you in the back. Can't do it, boy. We got to go before more soldiers come around. Let's git." After seeing them pick off those soldiers without an ounce of guilt, I believed him. We got back on our horses and I was sweating like July. My heart was beating as if I'd run down to the creek and back. Levi looked over at me.

"Something wrong Bobby?"

"Well, both of you seem like good soldiers, but I just remembered that my Pa's sick and I need to go home and take care of him and my Ma. I may need to wait a year or two and then I can come back and join up."

Reuben's face turned dark and he leaned forward in his seat. "You think we're going to let you just ride with us and then quit? We'll—" but Levi spoke up. He didn't sound like he was mad. In fact, he almost sounded like he'd expected me to act that way.

"That's okay Bobby. You can go. Because we know who you are and where you live. We'll find you and your folks and then we'll enjoy your Ma cooking a nice dinner for us. Now get before I change my mind."

Reuben looked at him real fast and this time Levi shook his head side to side. I just sat there looking, not sure what to do. Levi's smile was gone and his eyes narrowed, "Git!"

I've never been so scared in my life as I headed back home, especially those first fifty yards. I'd have bet all I had they were going to shoot me in the back. I was waiting for it. I wanted to look back so bad to see if their guns were raised. I didn't feel better until I made a turn around a bend and then peeked behind me. Course they were nowhere in sight, but that didn't mean they were gone. After that I kept looking around to see if they were following me. Every sound I heard I thought was them coming through the woods. It was awful.

I didn't write you for a few months because I didn't know how you'd take it. Ma kept wanting me to write and said she would if I didn't. Saying it wasn't fair for you not to know. So I'm sorry about that too.

I hope you can forgive me and that you'll write back. Like I said, I'm sorry.

Jimmy

November 24th, 1863

Dear John,

I'm so happy that Jimmy came back and wasn't hurt. I'm sure you're mad at him, but at least he's still alive. You can knock some sense into him when you get home. These are difficult times for young boys like him who feel like they can fight the world on their own and want to prove themselves. Just don't be too hard on him.

Pa spent an afternoon with the preacher the other day, and so afterwards I asked Pa why God let Winnie die. I quoted him a verse from Jeremiah, "For I know the thoughts that I think toward you, saith the Lord, thoughts of peace, and not evil, to give you an expected end." Pa said God only promised to save our souls, not to be happy. He said he asked the preacher if God knew what it was like to watch his daughter die right in from of him and not do anything about it. The preacher said, "I don't know about a daughter, but He knows about losing a son."

I was talking with a woman from our church the other day and she said her son was a nurse. She said on the one side it was rough because he was busy after a battle but at least he wasn't on a field just waiting to get shot. Would you consider being a medical nurse? I don't know how the army works and whether you could sign up for a spell or not but I'd appreciate it. I just don't want anything bad to happen to you. I don't want you to run away. I want this war to be over and for you to be here. Just think about it?

Love,
Annie

November 24th, 1863
Knoxville, TN

Dear Jimmy,

I can't believe you were with a couple of Champ Ferguson's men, if they really were with him. He's just a thief and a murderer and if he's caught he'll be hanged. I'm not going to write all of the possible bad endings you could've had. Just be thankful in your prayers at night that God sent an angel to keep you safe. Many, many young men have not been so lucky. That was clever to use Bobby's name. The little rat will almost deserve it if they ever come around.

I can't write about soldiering to Annie because she wants me to be a nurse, but I'll still write to you so I won't forget everything after the war. Just make sure and keep these letters safe.

We're still in Loudon, but I don't know how much longer we'll be here. On the morning of the 14th Longstreet came across the Tennessee River at Huff's Ferry. We were ordered to retreat to Knoxville, but as we headed there, Burnside met us and told us to turn around. The 9th Corps was joining us to push Longstreet back. So we marched all day long but basically didn't go anywhere. The worst part was the rain. Sometimes it was just a sprinkle, but other times it came down hard. It made the roads a mess, which makes the march that much harder. We were all trying not to fall, as it would make the whole company slow down and get tangled up. And of course there's the wagons. They'll get stuck any place they possibly can and then whoever's standing next to it gets ordered to push. I don't know how, but Pole and I always seem to be near the one that gets stuck the most. If you weren't dirty before you helped, you're covered in mud when you finish. And it's not like you can just walk down to the creek and wash off. You have to get back in line.

Sometime during the night Burnside received orders to send us back to Knoxville. So we marched back along the same muddy road, except this time the secesh met up with us and we had skirmishes around Lenoir Station. We paired up with the 107th Illinois. We were the last two regiments, keeping a distance between us and the Johnnies. When they got too close, we had to knock them back a bit. We started after them and chased them for a couple of miles before realizing they were up on a wooded hill, firing at us standing in an open field. Well, we weren't just going to let them have easy shots, so we charged up and drove them out. I know I hit a couple early on and then I thought I got one at the end, but Pole thought he hit the same rebel. A heavy-set fella wearing a brown, droopy hat. He stood out because he was having trouble firing his gun. Something wasn't working right on it and he was holding it this way and that, but he wasn't shooting. He caught our eye because that made him different than the rest. We argued for a little while about who hit him, but not for long. Pole and I aren't putting notches on our guns. We just want to win the war and go home. But it was me.

That was the longest night I can remember. We were hungry and thirsty after marching and fighting all day. We couldn't eat or drink anything because we weren't allowed to get into our knapsacks. We couldn't lie down either. We had to stand the whole night without building a fire and there was a heavy fog, so we stood there shaking in the cold with our loaded guns. For a while, everyone strained to see if we could hear or see anything coming out of the woods. I remember hearing footsteps coming through the leaves, just sure it was going to be a covey of rebels. Our company was loaded and ready to pour it on. With every crunch of the leaves they felt closer and closer, but it seemed like they were never going to come out of the woods. I wasn't closest to the woods but I heard someone laugh and say, "It's a family of coons!" We all shook our heads and took a deep breath.

We don't have too many fights at night because we'd end up shooting each other as much as we would the enemy. But when the other side is losing, you never know what he may try. Finally, daybreak came and we were given the order to fall back to Knoxville. But by now the roads were so torn up we had to leave some of the wagons behind. They wouldn't budge no matter how many of us pushed and pulled. I heard those mule drivers call those mules everything but a milk cow, but it wasn't any use. We carried all the goods we could, but what we couldn't carry we had to burn. It's awful sad to have to do this, but if we didn't then the enemy would get it and that's worse than burning.

There's been some light fighting every day with the rebels close behind us, and especially once we settled into Knoxville. There were some rebel sharpshooters who dug a rifle pit just outside our walls and they were picking off some of our soldiers now and then. A boy would be talking or looking around and then he'd either scream or just fall back dead. A regiment with the Second Michigan was ordered to take care of those sharpshooters. Our men ran out, but they were fired upon, and when they got to the pit they found more than they'd bargained for. The Johnnies were in the woods waiting for them and fired without mercy. Less than half of our soldiers came back alive. Now their sharpshooters target our officers. Three days ago a lieutenant was giving out orders and in the middle of his talking he just fell over. Graveyard dead. He never knew it.

There's also been some of ours disappear while on picket duty. The enemy will open fire on our lines and while we're trying to figure out where it's coming from, one of their regiments will come in and scoop up our pickets. It's scary now when the finger points to you for duty. David Cullen is a boy from an Illinois regiment I met around the campfire a few weeks ago. A while back David was getting ready to go on picket. He told me that if he got caught to mail a letter for him. At first I didn't want to take it.

"Mail it yourself when you're back tomorrow morning" I said.

Then he gave me a look. It reminded me of Papa just before I left to be mustered, when he said, "Don't be a fool and don't be a coward." At the time I didn't think it was very good advice. Who wants to be known as a fool or a coward? I understand why he said that now. Anyway, I took the letter and he looked me in the eye and thanked me. I mailed it today. I waited a week after he didn't come back. We don't know for sure, but we think he was caught, which I guess is as good as dead.

I don't know of a private who's been caught and escaped. No one knows what happens to them. Course there's all kinds of tales about sending them to prisons, or even working them in the cotton fields like slaves, but no one really knows. I was glad I took the letter, but sad I had to mail it with his belongings. We try to mail out all the letters a man kept as well as anything personal that his family might like to have. David was a good soldier.

On the morning of the 29th, the enemy decided to attack our works. We'd dug trenches and burned down every house in the area where we thought they could hide, but this wasn't meant to be a sneak attack. It had been a cold morning with light frost and a heavy, white fog all around. We heard them fire, but the fog dampened the sound. Instead of sounding like rifles, it sounded more like Papa cracking his knuckles. Still, we knew what was coming and we all got ready. There weren't the loud rebel yells like normal. In fact, there wasn't any yelling at all. We could only hear their sergeants keeping their men in rhythm with "hep, hep, hep, hep" and the stomping of thousands of feet as they marched up the hill double-quick. That's just a little slower than a flat-out run.

Once we saw them break out of the fog, we let them have it. After what seemed like a few minutes our rifles were hot enough to cook breakfast. We were given the "fire at will" to go as fast as we could. They fell, but they kept coming. We had a telegraph wire, or tangle, which ran across the clearing, and it was still early so they couldn't see it. Well, the first column tripped over it and then the next tripped over them until they were a mess, all the while making it easier for us to get them.

The ones who cleared the wire found a ditch before reaching our walls. Several jumped in, but none walked out. I was standing next to Pole and at one point I noticed neither of us were firing. We were both looking at these men continue to take steps forward, even though they knew they were going to die. Seeing those men fighting from the ditch and knowing they were all going to get it, one of our officers stood on the wall and asked if they'd surrender. They screamed their rebel yell and three shots went through the officer's jacket. Believe it or not, he was fine. But then one of the other officers got a 20-pound cannonball with a 5 second fuse. He lit it and threw it into the ditch. It exploded and the screams changed. Next we heard, "We surrender! We surrender!" That day the enemy lost 129 killed and 459 wounded. I later learned that these were Longstreet's picket brigades. Men who had won their battles at Gettysburg and Chickamauga. They didn't know how to lose and so they didn't retreat until too many of them were heaped on the ground.

We enjoyed the spoils of war just like at Pittsburgh Landing and Chaplin Hills. In the ditch they were piled at least three deep with some of the wounded suffering beneath the dead. It had been a while since I'd seen that. I hope I never see it again. Many men were shot through the head. Others had all sorts of limbs blown off. These days, more than others, I wish I could be home, crawl into my bed with the covers up to my neck and just stay there.

Looking past the bodies, this is a smart victory for the Union. Lincoln has wanted East Tennessee for some time but we were never able to make it happen till now. It's an important link for them between Virginia and the rest of the South and now it's broken. We hope that will make life harder on the enemy. Sooner or later they're going to have to realize we're going to win. I hope it's sooner.

Take care,
Johnny

December 8, 1863

Johnny,

Sounds like you've had it rough, although not as bad as some of the rebels. You don't have to worry about me. I've learned my lesson. I still think about those two Federal picket soldiers that were shot. I couldn't make out their faces, but I could tell they were squirming on the ground. They never knew what hit them either. I felt so sorry for them. Like when I killed that robin when I was little. I didn't think about it being a songbird. I was just proud I hit it. Ma didn't yell at me, but she let me know that little bird would never sing again.

I guess you see the stars most every night. I don't usually pay them too much attention but the other night I would've sworn the moon was so big I could've hit it with a rock. I know I could've read your letters without even lighting a candle. It was a sight to see.

I'm keeping up with your letters and they'll be here when you get back. You don't have to worry about that.

Jimmy

December 21st, 1863

Dear Annie,

I'm sorry it took so long for me to reply to your last letter. I've been frightful busy and really haven't had time for the last few weeks. I'm writing you from Tennessee still, letting you know that I won't be back in Kentucky for Christmas.

Well, you got your wish that I worked as a nurse, although it's not as easy or safe as it sounds. I'd rather be back on the line with my friends than nursing. We had some fighting and they needed more nurses so I tried it. I'm not going to write about the details but I'll just say that either I'll be coming home with all of my limbs or not at all. But at least I tried it. More than ever when I'm in a place like that I think of sitting with you on your porch. That's when I'm grateful for your cross. I can hold it and know that you've held that cross in your hand. It's funny that a little piece of metal means so much to me but I wouldn't trade it for anything. Even if it did almost get me killed.

I gave you that little package before I left for your Christmas present. I was hoping I'd be back to see you open it, but that's not going to happen. I hope you like it. Who knows, maybe this will be our last Christmas apart?

I was thinking. Maybe you and your folks could meet my folks even before the war's over? I could ask them to come to your house if you'd be agreeable. I know that once they meet you they'll love you. And when you meet them, you'll love my folks. I can't promise anything about Jimmy. If so then let me know of a weekend that'd be best, probably a Saturday before planting starts. If you don't want to that's fine. But since our folks don't know each other it'd be a chance for them to visit. If your folks agree then please send a letter to Jimmy Gore in Hardyville.

> When you see me coming, raise your window high.
> When I'm a leaving, I'll hang my head and cry.

Merry Christmas to you and your family.

Take care,
John

December 20th, 1863
Knoxville, TN

Dear Jimmy,

After the Knoxville battle there were plenty of wounded all over the place. A few weeks ago Pole and I happened to be standing next to our sergeant when a captain came up and ordered him to transfer two men from his regiment to the medical corps. The captain had a signed letter and gave it to the sergeant. Well, I was looking right at the sergeant while this conversation was happening and he turned to the officer and said, "Yes sir, Captain, I have just the right men for you. They have a particular interest in the medical field." I remember thinking to myself, "That's funny, I've never heard of anybody asking to be in the medical corps." Then the sergeant looked at Pole and me and said, "C'mon you two, pack your belongings and get going!" We knew there was no point in arguing. We'd been in the army long enough to know that when you're ordered to do something you'd better just go ahead and saddle up. Complaining just makes it worse.

Neither Pole nor I had any idea what would happen. All of us try to avoid the tents with the yellow flag and the green "H," afraid we'll be worse coming out than going in. The medical training was quick. We were taught how to change the dressings, give out medicines, and assist in surgery. But just like when you asked about all the different words we used as soldiers, there's plenty that we use in the medical tent too. Since we had to learn so much so fast, I'm glad I'm writing this down, because I'm liable to forget most of it.

We learned how to spot shirkers trying to get a free ticket home and avoid fighting. There's several terms I've heard like "skulker" and "turnspit," or when they're "trying to play off" so that they can get out of battle. Some are just lazy and try to stay in the sick tent as long as they can, so we call them "hospital buzzards."

But I met a boy the other day and I still don't have him figured out. By looking at him, he ought to be able to get out and fight, but he says he can't do it anymore. I waited till the other nurses and surgeons went away and I came back and talked to him. It took me a while, but I finally said, "They're coming for you tomorrow and if you don't fight, then you're as good as dead."

He looked up at me and said, "Then let me die, but I can't go in a battle again. I just can't. I'd rather they hang me now."

It didn't make any sense to me. I said, "But if you fight, you have a chance of living. I've fought several times and I'm still here. I don't like fighting and I know I could get hit whenever the Good Lord decides to call me home but at least I have a chance. Why would you give up and die?" When I finished asking my last question he started looking at the floor. He shook his head side to side and looked up at me with tears coming out of both eyes. I'll never forget what he said.

"You think I want it to end like this? You think I want everyone to call me a coward and my family to be ashamed of me. I wish I could go out there and get in line like the rest of you, but I can't. I wish I knew why or how to fix it, but there ain't no fix. The only fix is for me to die in front of a firing line or at the end of a rope. I never thought my life would end this way.

But I ain't got no choice. I can't go back into battle. So this is how I'm going to go out. And there ain't nobody that can help me, except Lincoln." A couple of soldiers came and took him the following day. I don't know where exactly. I heard he was sent to a prison and waiting to see if the president would pardon him. The man who told me said that the president had pardoned a lot of men for not fighting. He felt the president should use them as bait in a big battle. They'd get killed, but they should die anyway and this way their families could at least feel proud of them for something. I know for the boy that was taken away, Taylor was his last name, the only way he'd go out on a field is hog tied. He wouldn't go out just because someone had a gun pointed towards him. I don't know what to do with him, but I don't think he should be hanged or shot. Now for men who are lazy and sorry, I agree with sending them into a battle where the fighting is the roughest.

It's not as easy as it sounds, figuring out the ones who are trying to get out of fighting. But when you look at it like a game, it can almost be fun. When someone claims to be deaf you can fire a gun behind him while he is sleeping and watch him wake up confused. Before the war this may not have been as fair because if you're really asleep and if the gun is a rod or two away, you may not hear it. But any man who's been in battle wakes up the second he hears a gunshot. Another man may act paralyzed in his legs, but give him anesthesia (medicine that makes him go to sleep) and when he's coming out of it he'll move all his limbs fine. Blindness can be difficult to prove too. There's one type of blindness that soldiers get that's called "graveled." It comes on quick after a long march but it's usually only blindness at night, not during the day. But a shirker will act like he's blind until hardtack is thrown at his face when he's not expecting it. It's really hard not to squint or turn his head a little. This may seem harsh, but after cleaning up the spoils of war a few times, neither Pole nor myself feel sorry for cowards.

Still, most of the men here really are sick. We see a lot of soldiers with what we call "Camp Fever." After working for a few days you can spot them in ten seconds. Those poor men get the Tennessee high step, a certain way they walk when they have diarrhea. Usually the poor devils get a little opium, which helps some, but they're as weak as kittens if they make it. And many don't. I would've never believed it when I joined, but some of the older nurses told me that more men die from diarrhea than bullets. The condition is so bad that sometimes the surgeons are called "loose bowels" because it seems that's all they treat. Then there's other illnesses men get by visiting a fancy lady, so-called "diseases of indulgence." These men are in bad shape, although there's not much we do for them. Working in the hospital tent for a week and seeing these wretches pass through would keep most men from going to those houses. The surgeons give them special blue pills. I've helped make a batch before and know it has mercury, chalk, licorice, and honey. I don't know if those pills help or not, but the surgeons give them to every sick soldier who can swallow. When we're handing them out some call it "Blue Mass."

But treating diarrhea and the like are not why being a nurse is the worst job in the army. When you're marching through a field, listening to your sergeant bark orders, you think about getting shot and your friends getting shot, but when someone falls you don't stop. I stopped for Scrap for a few seconds, but later when someone fell I just kept going. It's what you have to do. If everybody stopped then we wouldn't be firing, and if we aren't firing then more of us die. As infantry we considered the medical corps easy since you're less likely to get shot, a "featherbed fighter" some say. But it's not so. I talked to some of the nurses who go out into the fields during battle and many of them are injured while carrying someone back. The musicians sometimes carry the wounded as nurses after playing the music to get us into battle. I always thought they had an easy job too, until now.

Once shots are fired and soldiers start to fall, the nurses go out in twos and check those on the ground. They decide who'll live and who'll die. Those that aren't going to last very long are taken to a big tree near the field. This becomes the dying tree. One nurse, Isaiah was his name, a big man with square shoulders, was telling me about going through the wounded on the field. He said taking men to the dying tree was the worst part, or at least turning around and walking away was. He didn't like the idea that he was the one who decided which men lived and which died. He hadn't had any real medical training, just what he picked up in the army. He felt it was too much sometimes, so if there was any chance a boy might make it, he'd take them back. Every so often a surgeon would complain about filling up their beds with dead men, but Isaiah said he'd rather bring a hundred dead men back than leave one at the tree who could've made it.

Those that are chosen to go to the hospital tent are loaded onto a stretcher, which is two long sticks tied to a blanket. Sometimes they'll put the wounded onto a two-wheeled cart called a "Hop, Step, and a Jump." If your back didn't hurt before you rode in one, it would afterwards. I think you could make butter just by sitting the churn in the cart for a few trips. Next they load the wounded onto what they call the "dead cart," which is a small wagon that goes to the medical tent. They usually don't call it that when a soldier's on it.

Once in the tent, the surgeons (or, as they're known in camp, "sawbones") take a look at the wounded and decide on surgeries. A belly wound means sure death within a few days and the surgeons won't even bother. A chest shot either seems to die within a few minutes or sometimes lives a few days. Most of the wounds are shots to the arms and legs and for these there's only one option. Amputate. Once the younger surgeons make a casualty list, or "butcher's bill" as we call it, they start to line the wounded up. This is where I come in. I help carry the men onto the tables and then hold them down while someone gets a cup with some medicine in it that puts them to sleep. I've heard there's been times when they didn't have the medicine and they'd have to give the wounded a swig of Nockum Stiff or whatever whiskey they have. Sometimes they just have to give a man a bullet to bite on. I'd seen bullets with teeth marks in them before and now I know where they came from.

"Better to lose a limb than a life" is a saying I've heard a dozens of times from the surgeon. I hope we're doing these men favors by cutting off their arms and legs. There was one soldier, from Ohio I think, who kept his pistol and threatened any nurse or doctor who tried to take off his arm with a bullet in the head. At first one of the surgeons, a tall, heavy, bald man named Dr. Thompson, argued with him, but eventually he said the soldier could "die with his arm and good riddance." Eventually the arm healed and the man did fine.

But there was another boy brought in who'd been shot in his leg. I hadn't been there long, but even I knew what was in store for him. Trouble was, he knew too. His name was Paul Marcrum. He had blue eyes and even though he was about my age, he had some gray in his hair. As he told me later, he was charging with his regiment in an advance and was shot. He thought he'd been stung by a bee at first, but then his leg gave out and he went down. Once on the ground he pulled up his pant leg to see the blood pouring out of his calf. He tried to tie a cloth around it and walk, but he fell again and this time someone called for a nurse. He didn't want to go, but they showed him the advancing rebels. He knew if he was still there when they came they'd spear him. He agreed and was taken to our tent. Before they brought him in, one of the nurses tied a cloth real tight above the shot. That nurse used a stick to make it so tight that Paul was complaining about it, but Dr. Thompson said the tourniquet saved his life.

Once he realized where he was, Paul was shaking. One of the younger surgeons told him it was from losing so much blood, but I think it was from fear of the surgery more than anything else. He started stammering and begging us to not take off his leg and then he went quiet. I was tending to him and thought he wasn't going to say any more, but as I was just about to turn and leave, he looked at me and asked, "How am I ever going to plow a field with one leg, or work a farm, or find a wife? What woman's going to want a man with only one good leg?" I didn't argue with him. I shrugged my shoulders and gave a slight smile. If I'd tried to talk with him I'd start stuttering and then he'd either make fun of me or feel sorry for me. And I didn't need either.

I've heard other men at night around the campfire say that if their leg gets shot they'll just go ahead and finish the job themselves so they're not spending the rest of their life depending on anybody. I had thought about it a little after Pittsburgh Landing, but after a few days in the medical tent, I had more time than I wanted to think about what life would be like for me with only one good arm or leg. Course I'd like to think Annie would still take me even if I was lame, but I wouldn't know till it happened. Besides, would it even be fair to ask her to hitch herself to a lame husband that can't do a full day's work? Before I met Annie and worked in the medical tent, I never worried about it. But after seeing men like Paul, I realized it could just as easy have been me on that blanket thinking about my leg. Except poor Paul didn't have a gun. Dr. Thompson came in, looked at the leg, then he looked at us and nodded. And that was it. He didn't have to say anything. We all knew to get ready for surgery. Paul looked like a trapped rabbit and kept asking, "What's gonna happen?"

I felt so bad for Paul. I wanted to explain, but couldn't. Dr. Thompson and the other surgeon didn't care enough to talk to him. They discussed how they were going to operate right in front of him, but had no actual concern for Paul. He kept asking the same question and they acted like he was a pig getting ready for slaughter, talking amongst themselves but ignoring him. As we were lifting him up to the table, he tried to squirm off, but he didn't have any luck. We've had to hold men down so many times, we're pretty good at it.

I thought that after a couple of years in the army I knew what cursing was, but let me tell you. When a man's being tied down to have his leg or his arm cut off and he doesn't want to lose it, he'll call you everything he can think of and sometimes things that don't even make sense. One older soldier was cursing at me and calling me all the usual names and I just ignored him. Finally he said, "You're nothing but a two-footed mouse!" I stopped what I was doing and looked at him and asked him what that meant. He just glared at me. He was so mad he couldn't speak. I'd never seen someone that angry before. Later I told that story and the other nurses laughed. Except Pole. Neither of us agree with how the soldiers are treated, but there's nothing we can do.

Once the cup of medicine was put over Paul's face, his arms and legs relaxed. Dr. Thompson started sharpening his blades. The work was quick and in a few minutes he was sewing up what was left of Paul's leg. We took the scraps and threw them in a pile outside with the rest of the day's work. The first time I saw the pile of hands and feet I got sick on the spot, but after just a week it didn't bother me anymore. I could sit and eat next to it now. After Paul's operation was finished, the surgeon wiped his blade on his apron and moved to the next man. This happened again and again and again until all in the hospital were fixed.

As he was waking, Paul groaned in pain. Then he sat up and saw the bandages and the empty place where his foot should have been. At first he didn't say anything, he just fell back in bed with his arms over his eyes. He wouldn't eat and didn't talk much for the first couple of days, but then he started complaining of how his leg was hurting worse. I'd been dressing his wound with bandages dipped in turpentine, which is how we do it, but it didn't look right. I asked Dr. Thompson to look at his tap, or what some call a stump. It smelled rotten and looked red and swollen. The surgeon said the inflammation was coming out and it looked good. Paul finally tried to eat the thin chicken broth we call "shadow soup" but he was getting weaker. He was asking for morphine as often as we could give it to him. It helps make the pain go away for a while.

A couple of days later the swelling was so bad the stitches were bursting and what came out was this awful, yellow mess. There were red streaks going up his leg. This time Dr. Thompson said more surgery was needed to clean the leg. Now normally Dr. Thompson acts like he's the smartest one in the room and we all need to know it, but his head was a little lower this time around. Paul didn't fight getting on the table because of the pain. I remember he was breathing fast. After the surgery Paul groaned, but he didn't say anything that made sense. Dr. Thompson came by and poked at the wound till Paul screamed in pain. Without looking anyone in the eye the surgeon said, "Keep him comfortable. The wound was too bad to begin with, he never had a chance." And he walked away. Paul slept and moaned for a couple of days, but one time he woke up and knew who he was and who I was. He looked up at me and grabbed hold of my shirt.

"Please don't let me die. I don't care if I do only have one good leg, just don't let me die. Please help me."

I looked into his eyes and nodded. I buried him the next day.

At least I knew the name to put on Paul's marker. Too many others die without anybody knowing their names, they're just called "Somebody's Darling" and buried with a blank cross. I remember burying men after Pittsburgh Landing and feeling like we should have a church service for each one, like if they'd died at home. I'd look into a man's eyes, if he still had them, and try to remember if I'd known him. When I'm on burying duty now, I don't look at the faces. I just treat it as a chore, except instead of Papa telling me, it's an officer. It's easier to get to sleep if you don't look at the face.

A corporal told me yesterday that Pole and I were set to get transferred back to our unit next week. I can't wait. I may get shot or worse, but it beats this. Being a nurse isn't nearly as easy as I thought it was. I just pray I never have to see the inside of one of these tents again.

I wish you could mail me a Christmas dinner, but at least try to get me a little tobacco. Pretty soon you and Ma can open the presents I sent you a while back. It's not much, just something I picked up. Merry Christmas and Happy New Year!

By the way, I asked Annie about you and the folks going over to her house to meet her and her family sometime soon. She's the one for me. I know it. We're meant to be together.

Take care,
Johnny

December 29th, 1863

Dear Jimmy,

My name is Annie Elzey. I hope you've heard as much about me as I have of you. I wanted to invite you and your folks to visit my family for dinner. Either the second or third Saturday in January would be fine if it doesn't snow. We live about ten miles outside of town off of Smith Ridge Road in Campbellsville. Our house is set off the road a piece with a red barn next to it. There's three large oaks in the front.

I hope to meet you soon,
Annie

December 30th, 1863

Johnny,

I guess I hadn't really given much thought to what nurses did. I knew they tended to the sick and helped the doctors, but I had no idea what it was really like. And the newspaper never talks about it like you. It will say the doctors worked really hard to save men's lives. But they never talk about them cutting off arms and legs as fast as they can.

We opened your gifts. Ma really liked the little sugar bowl. I'd never seen metal so soft before. I was mashing it a little this way and that until she hit me over the head to stop. Where'd you get it? I noticed it had Toothill on the bottom.

I liked my jackknife too. I'd been packing one of Papa's old knives, but didn't have one of my own. Papa got me a piece of whetstone and showed me how to spit when I'm sharpening it. I just have to be careful not to cut myself on account of keeping it too sharp. I carry it around everywhere I go except to bed. And then it's by the lamp. We sent you a package too. I hope you got it.

Christmas was gray and cold, but no snow. We had a big supper and of course we all wished you could've been here. Thomas and his family came by. I swear those kids grow an inch every time I see them now. Ma keeps telling Little Russell she's going to put a brick on his head. He looks at her and tilts his head to the side, like she just may do it.

I hope you had a good Christmas and next year you'll be here.

I said something to Ma about visiting Annie and her folks. She paused for a bit, raised her eyebrows and said, "That'd be fine if that's what he wants."

Jimmy

| G | 13 | Ky. |

John J. C. Gore

Prt., Co. A, 13 Reg't Kentucky Infantry.

Appears on

Company Muster Roll

for Nov. & Dec., 1863.

Present or absent absent,

Stoppage, $ 100 for

Due Gov't, $ 100 for

Remarks: Detached as
nurse in Hospital
since Dec. 7th 1863.

Book mark:

(358) Ash luling Copyis.

Chapter Eleven

January 4th, 1864

Dear John,

Thank you so much for the bowl. It's very pretty and I've already been using it to keep my pins. I wish I would have given you your gift before you left, but I guess I'll have to wait until you get back to Kentucky. I've heard not to send anything valuable to a soldier as someone might steal it. Don't worry. I'll take care of it for you.

After my last letter my folks asked questions about us. They wanted to know if it was serious and I told them it was. We talked for a while and I think all you have to do is ask Pa and he'll say yes. I was scared Ma would say I'm her only daughter now and wouldn't want me to leave, but I think she's more afraid that I'll be an old maid. Besides, with the war there's not as many young men as there used to be and when it's over there's going to be some girls without a husband. I love the idea of meeting your family. I sent a letter to Jimmy for them to come over the first or second or third week of January. We'll be looking for them.

I've never been so happy for a year to start. Before this year is finished you'll be done with your fighting and we'll be closer to starting a life together. At least our house isn't as quiet as it has been. A few weeks ago just as we were finishing supper, Pa told us that it was okay to say Winnie's name. That she was a happy little girl and she wouldn't want us to be sad the rest of our lives. I started crying and Ma started crying and even Pa started crying. If the rebels would've walked in on us they would've left us alone as we were a sorry looking bunch. But it was like a break in the clouds. We've been talking a lot more and I think it's going to be alright.

I'm sorry being a nurse didn't work out, but at least you tried. More than anything else, I want you to be safe and come home. I'm glad you still like the cross and that it's helped you. Oh, I can hardly wait for your time to be up and this silly war to be over! I wish it were already next year so much.

> Peach tree bark and apple tree sap,
> If you want me, then you'll have to ask Pap.

Love,
Annie

January 8th, 1864

Dear Annie,

My folks and I thank you for inviting us to come visit. I've heard your fried chicken is really good. It looks like we'll be able to come over the third Saturday in January, the 16th. We look forward to meeting you.

Jimmy

January 12th, 1864
Knoxville, TN

Dear Jimmy,

I know you're not going to get this letter right away but I couldn't wait to write it.

I'm glad you liked the knife. It's just like the ones we use. They're considered so basic to a soldier that I'm told in prison they sometimes let men keep them. Ma's sugar bowl is pewter, which is why it's so soft. It was made in Sheffield, England by a Robert Toothill and shipped over here. At least that's what the sutler told me, but then again they lie. We call the area where the sutlers sell their wares "Robber's Row" for a reason. Anyway, I thought it was different and Ma would like it.

You're really gonna like this next part. I was sitting around the campfire yesterday eating dinner next to some boys from other states. Depending on what we're doing, we usually don't have a big breakfast or dinner, but eat a lot for supper, since we have more time to cook it. For dinner we usually just have some hardtack and beans that have been cooking since breakfast. Anyway, I was sitting and talking with a boy and turns out he was from Ohio. He had been in Munfordville for a spell with his regiment. So then I asked if he had gone around to different farms there. He said that with all of the traitors in the area, they had a lot of problems with the locals tearing up tracks and blowing up bridges. I asked if he'd ever been to a farm where they claimed to have a son fighting for the Union. He said several of them did that, but they didn't pay them any mind, cause that's what they'd expect traitors to say.

He said he remembered one farm with an older couple and a younger son and that his sergeant in particular didn't like that family. He figured if they went back there his sergeant was going to make the younger son join their regiment. I asked if his sergeant had a black beard with a grey stripe. He tucked his chin back and said, "That's an odd question. Why yes, he does. How in the world did you guess that?" I didn't answer but got up and started walking. I thought I might have heard him yell, "Wait!" but I didn't care. I went over to where his regiment's colors and camp were. It didn't take long before I saw Sergeant Skunky. I wanted to go up and knock him down but I knew better. I just had to make sure it was him.

I went to Sergeant Hickman and told him the story. He asked if I was sure that the sergeant was the same one that bothered you all and I nodded my head. He then took me to see the colonel and the sergeant told the story with me nodding. The colonel was looking at a paper until the part that Ma was knocked down, then he looked up at the sergeant and then at me. The colonel asked the sergeant in front of me, "Sergeant, I believe that Private Gore has been a good soldier for the 13th, isn't that right?" I'll admit I was a little nervous by the question. The sergeant's never told any of us how we've done to a man. I was thinking about how I'd done as a soldier. I hadn't done anything bad enough to be punished, but I hadn't done anything especially brave, either. It seemed like a long pause.

Finally the sergeant said, "Yes sir. He's a fine soldier who follows orders. In fact, I was going to speak to you about his promotion to corporal. He wouldn't be fit to command men on the field, but I think he could work in supply." I couldn't believe it. The sergeant never looked at me but just stared straight at the colonel.

The colonel nodded, got up from his chair and said, "Well, that's what I thought. You two come with me." We then followed him to the Ohio colonel's tent. Colonel Hobson told us to wait outside while he entered. I remembered that just before he went into the tent he paused for a few seconds, like he was gathering his thoughts. We weren't inside the tent but we could hear. He told the other colonel our story and asked why his troops were attacking his soldiers' families. "And don't tell me cause you can't tell them apart! If you can't, then leave them alone." I'd never heard the colonel get excited like that. The Ohio colonel didn't have a response and then Colonel Hobson said that if it happened again he would request harsh punishment for that sergeant. "And I don't mind asking Grant or Lincoln for that matter."

The colonel exited the tent with wide eyes. He looked at me and asked, "Where's this sergeant?" I led the way to where he was half an hour before. I felt like a fox clearing the way for a giant bear. The colonel was all worked up so I knew now was the best time to get the sergeant. And there he was. As soon as I pointed him out to the colonel, the colonel walked straight to him and all of the soldiers stood up at attention. The sergeant stood and saluted the colonel. The colonel didn't return the salute but asked him about going to different houses around Hardyville, in particular a house where the mother stated her son was fighting for the 13th. The sergeant stuttered and said, "I don't remember sir, maybe, yes, I think so." The colonel took a deep breath and then gave the sergeant a tongue lashing like I'd never heard. He ended it with, "If I ever hear that you've attacked the farms of any of my soldiers again, I'll take it out in your hide, sergeant. Your hide. You understand me, sergeant?" The sergeant stood there at attention and said a very soft, "Yes sir." He was still saluting the colonel while the colonel walked away. I looked at the sergeant and he looked at me. I gave him a little smile, not a friendly one, mind you. But a "My colonel will take care of me. You may outrank me, but he outranks you" smile. That was the best day I've had in quite a while. Ma always says it's wrong to want revenge, but I think it's okay to want what's right.

I don't know how much longer we'll be here in Knoxville. I guess till the rebels leave us alone. We hear they're worse off than us. That they're hungry and don't have clothes fit to wear. But they're still there. So we just wait it out.

Let me know how it goes with meeting Annie's family. I know you'll behave yourself.

Take care,
Johnny

January 17th, 1864

Dear John,

I loved meeting your family, even Jimmy. You're like your Pa. He's quiet and doesn't speak much but when he does it's either good advice or really funny. Sometimes it's hard to know when he's being serious or funny so I have to wait for him to give a little smile or wink. Your Ma is so sweet and happy. Jimmy minded his manners the whole time. He didn't talk much but he sure could eat.

My Ma had cleaned our house three times over. She was washing everything so much I thought she was going to ask me to clean the bird droppings off the roof. Then she was scared the food wasn't going to turn out right, but it was all fine. Saturday afternoon my Pa was nervous too, refilling and lighting his pipe every few minutes.

Thank goodness for your Ma. She put everyone at ease with talking and laughing. Without her I think the rest of us might of just stood around and looked at each other. Once we introduced ourselves then the menfolk went outside and we stayed in the house. I don't know why, by my Ma wasn't exactly saying the nicest things about me. "Annie is a pretty good cook. I mean, her fried chicken isn't as good as mine, but it's tolerable." At first I wanted to hide then I just wanted her to hush. But your Ma was encouraging to me the whole time. All of your family made over how good the food was, which helped me take a deep breath and relax my shoulders for the first time in a week

After they left my Pa said your family was good people and Ma didn't say anything but nodded and her eyes got soft. I think everyone is happy for us to get married. That was a good idea for our folks to meet before you finish with the army. Now we won't have to wait as long.

Stay safe.

Love,
Annie

January 18ᵗʰ, 1864

Dear Annie,

I wanted to write and thank you and your folks for having us over a couple of days ago. We all felt that you're a really good cook and your family is very nice. My Ma thinks you and Johnny are going to be good together. My Pa thinks so too. I don't really know about that sort of thing but I wish you the best.

Jimmy

January 29th

Dear Jimmy,

Thank you very much for the letter. We loved having your family over and getting to visit. I wish I could've met the rest of your family but I'm sure I will soon. I'm glad you liked the chicken. I'm sure I'll be cooking it again for you in the future and you can eat as much as you like.

Annie

February 1st, 1864

Johnny,

I got your letter yesterday and I was so excited to read about your colonel giving it to Skunky I read it over and over again. And then I went to read it to Ma and Papa so they won't worry about anybody coming around here and bothering us anymore. I've thought of all the things I'd like to say to that Skunky, none of it nice, but I couldn't have said it better than your colonel. There's a part of me that would like to see the sergeant now, just to smile and know there's nothing he can do to me.

I set a trap last week and was hoping to catch a rabbit, but caught a raccoon instead. I'm curing his pelt. He was fat, too. I bet he was the one who ate the four rows of corn this fall. He won't be doing that again. Papa says I can make a nice, warm hat out of him, but I haven't decided.

We got word that Matthew Sowders from church got killed in Chattanooga. I don't know how he got with a different regiment, but he was one of those charging up the hill. Papa says it's called Missionary Ridge and that a lot of our men died. I'm sure you know about the battle, but I didn't know if you'd heard about Matthew. He was always so happy it's hard to think of him running up a hill and somebody killing him. I don't ever remember seeing him without a smile on his face. But he's gone. At least Grant won another battle. Papa says he'll get the rebels on the run and he won't let up, which is what we need.

You'll be happy to know we had a nice visit with the Elzeys. Ma and Papa liked Annie and her family right away. After we got there Papa and I went outside with her pa. Of course they talked about the usual things like weather, crops and critters. But her pa looked at ours and said in a real serious voice, "Those rebels killed my youngest daughter Winnie. I'd be proud to have a son-in-law who fought for the Federals." Papa didn't say anything but looked down and nodded his head. I didn't know what to do so I looked down too. Then all three of us were looking down when we heard a hawk flying over and there was a little bird chasing it away. Course the little bird always stays above the hawk. Then Papa told his story about seeing two foxes fight over a rabbit and while they were fighting a hawk came and took the rabbit away. Then we went back inside and ate.

I wrote Annie a letter to thank her family for having us over. And I told her how much I liked her fried chicken. That wasn't too hard though, she does make the best fried chicken I've ever had. I'll give you this, at least you picked a woman that can cook.

Jimmy

March 15th, 1864

Dear Jimmy,

I hope you and your family are doing good. I haven't heard from John for several weeks. I'm sure it's just slow mail because of the war, but I wanted to see if you'd received any letters from him?

Thanks,
Annie

March 23, 1863

Annie,

I haven't heard from Johnny since the middle of January, which is a long spell for him not to write. I'll bet it's just cause of where they're fighting. The mail probably isn't getting out. We'll hear from him directly.

By the way, I was talking with my pa the other day and I said your fried chicken was the best. He looked around to make sure my ma wasn't around and said, "You're right. Just don't tell Ma I said so. Maybe when she's part of the family she'll share her recipe."

Jimmy

| G | 13 | **Ky.** |

John J C Gore

Pvt., Co. A, 13 Reg't Kentucky Infantry.

Appears on

Company Muster Roll

for Jan and Feb, 1864.

Present or absent_____

Stoppage, $_____100 for_____

Due Gov't, $_____100 for_____

Remarks: Captured by Enemy
near Knoxville Jay 26. 64.
Had in possession one
Enfiel Rifle & accoutements
_____

M.O. roll next on which name
appears.

NEXT ROLL ON FILE, JUN 1864

Book mark:_____

B H Johnson

(358)   Copyist.

Chapter Twelve

START HERE
April 15th, 1864

Dear Jimmy,

Little brother how life has changed. I don't know what you've heard about me. I'm writing this letter to put these last few months on paper. I'm afraid if I don't, no one will know.

I know the paper looks like a mess, but it's because I had to write it cross-hatch. So once you finish this letter, you'll have to start back here and turn the paper one quarter turn to the right. I don't have much paper and we have to hide our letters. I sew mine into the lining of my clothes. You'll get to that in a bit. First let's start back at Knoxville.

It was January 26th and Pole and I were assigned picket duty for the night. We didn't want to go, but then nobody did. We all knew the risk of being out there with the rebels eager to pick off a few soldiers. Just as we started walking our route, a light, wet snow began to fall. It just covered the shorter blades of grass and then froze. The ground crunched. There were a few of us, and after we each walked our path, we'd meet in the middle where there was a fire. I remember Robert and Billy talking. I didn't really care what they were saying, just hearing the words. Pole was next to me and I don't think he was listening either. We were all a little sleepy with the cold air and the hot fire. Then *Crack!* A shot fired on us.

We knelt down and cocked back the hammers on our guns. We strained the darkness to catch a glimpse of where the shot had come from. Out of the corner of my eye I saw a few flashes to the right and heard the pops of the guns. I patted my chest to make sure I hadn't been hit. I didn't feel anything, but I'd heard enough stories of men who'd been shot and didn't know it for a minute. Next I looked in Pole's direction. I could just make out his face in the firelight. Pole's eyes were wide and staring straight ahead. Then he looked at me. It's the first time I'd ever seen him scared. He'd dropped his gun and his left hand was clutching his right arm. I threw down my gun to look at his wound. I knew the bullet hadn't cut a big artery because there wasn't enough blood. Still, a little red makes a big stain.

"I'm fine. Don't worry about it," Pole said. He was trying not to sound as scared as he was. Since Pole and I had both helped as nurses, we knew what happened to a man who was shot in the arm if a surgeon got ahold of him. Those poor boys on the tables begged us to let them go, but we couldn't. We both knew those were the darkest sins of our lives, much worse than shooting or even stabbing a rebel. We never said it, but I always thought my punishment for holding down those poor souls would be that one day somebody would hold me down. I bet Pole thought that too as he lay there holding his bloody arm.

Although the shot wasn't severe, it needed to be cleaned up. I looked over at Robert and ordered, "Take Pole and get help!" He didn't have to listen to me as I didn't outrank him, but he nodded his head and started to get up.

Pole argued, "I'm fine, just give me my gun!"

Then I said, "Raise your right arm."

Pole responded, "Well to be honest, I don't really feel like lifting it right now."

I looked over at Robert and he helped get Pole up on his feet. He gave me Pole's gun for an extra shot. Pole looked and said, "Alright, you can stay and cover us. Fire off a couple of rounds and then get out. See you in a bit."

As they were leaving I could see the brush move twenty yards away. I knew it was the rebels. I fired Pole's gun into the middle of it. I couldn't believe it but I got a hit. I could tell by the scream. Next I heard a few voices, then at least a dozen rebel soldiers came running out of the brush towards us, screaming and firing. Billy shot and then fell back with a bullet through his head. I fired my gun, but this time I missed. I had no more shots loaded and they were still coming. I knew how long it would take me to load another round, even at my fastest. There wasn't enough time.

Around the campfires, especially when we were just mustered in, everyone sat around and talked about how he would fight to the death. If we ran out of bullets then we'd charge with a bayonet. Better to die with honor than be taken prisoner. I looked at my gun, which didn't even have the bayonet fastened in place and saw no hope in charging. All I could think about was Annie. I saw her face with an awful sadness to it, crying as our dreams of making a life together were blown away. I couldn't take it. If I fought I was sure to die. But in prison there's a chance. At least you're alive. I dropped my gun and raised my arms.

When the rebels came up, one of them, about my age, wanted to shoot me anyway. Since I'd killed one of theirs, he felt it was fair. Then came an older rebel, he had more gray hairs than brown and said that I was to be taken prisoner and quartered. They argued for a while, but the older soldier won.

I was taken to their camp for a couple of days where I was tied to a tree and given water a couple of times. There was hardly any food for them and none for me. They put me together with other prisoners they'd captured and marched us north towards Virginia. There were at least thirty of us, but nobody knew where we were going and nobody asked a rebel. We were all taken from around Knoxville but I didn't know any of the others. There were a few boys that seemed to know each other well and they were talking about how we'd all be exchanged for rebel prisoners. One of them talked like he knew exactly how the trade would occur and his friend kept agreeing with him and saying, "That's what I heard, too!" The more they talked the more of us got interested and kept listening.

But finally an older soldier who had been keeping to himself said, "Fools! Look at our ranks. I'm the highest ranking soldier here and I'm just a corporal. We won't be exchanged for nothing. We're headed to a secesh prison. I've heard stories of officers being exchanged, but I ain't never heard of a private being released from a rebel prison. Make no mistake about it. Unless Grant wins the war in the next few months, ain't none of us going home this side of the grave. Don't believe me? How many of you ever heard stories of privates spending time in prison? Huh? Nobody, that's right! They don't get out. They go there and die and that's why there ain't no stories about them. Just like nobody will know about us!" Course then some of the other boys started arguing with him, but he just growled a little and never said anything after that. I didn't want to believe what he said was true, but I knew it was.

After several days of marching we were loaded onto a train. Light cracked through the walls here and there but it was mostly dark. We were kept in the cars for three days. I don't remember how many times we stopped but every time we did we would yell as loud as we could for them to let us out. They ignored us. Men had to mess themselves as there was no place to go. We were all cold and starving, and the smell would've turned a hog's stomach. When the door finally opened, the light was so bright I could hardly see. I remember being lined up in front of a large, brick building.

I was ordered up to the second floor. I'd never seen anything like it. Hundreds of men all packed into this room. I say men, but I'd never seen men so sick and thin before. I looked around for a familiar face but saw none. The open windows let cold breezes in every few seconds. I saw an open spot just under a window and sat down. After cleaning up battlefields and working as a nurse, I thought I'd seen the worst that one man can do to another. Now I realized all I'd done is break ground, here I was falling into a pit. Some of these men were walking ghosts. Their bodies were no more than skin stretched over bones with sunken eyes. I didn't say anything for a couple of days. I couldn't believe I was in such a place and did nothing but look around. I saw the dead being carried out, but not before their bodies were stripped of everything valuable. I'd never been lower. I tried to cry, but I couldn't. I didn't have enough water for tears. I asked a man next to me where I was and he looked straight ahead and answered, "You're in Richmond, son. Richmond, Virginia." I asked him the date and he said it was February 11th. I asked if he was sure and then he looked at me and said, "Course I'm sure. I asked a guard the day I got here twenty-two days ago. I've been keeping count." Then he stood up and left. I haven't talked to him since. It was the first I'd talked to anyone in days. He seemed like he'd lost his soul.

One day as I sat with my knees bent and my arms resting on my knees, I heard a scratchy, kind voice, "Hey there, where you from?" I turned and saw a man who well fed may have looked to be in his early fifties, but being as lean as he was looked much older. He had a smile on his face, which in that room was like a lantern in a cave. I told him who I was and how I got there. His name was Lewis Childers. He nodded his head and asked me questions about my family and if I had a wife. I told him I had a girl I'd been writing to but I hadn't spoken to her Pa. After telling him about Annie he nodded his head several times and said, "Good. That's good. That'll keep you alive three extra months at least. You do want to live, don't you?"

As you're reading this in your bed, that must seem like a strange question but I was sitting there looking at a room full of misery. Each man had to consider if he wanted to keep going or not and the answer wasn't always yes. But I said I did. His eyes squinted a bit, he leaned forward and then he spoke a little lower.

"Well then. We've heard tell that the rebels are looking for volunteers to go to a new prison they've just built. It's not in a large warehouse but out in the woods. They say there's a stream in the middle where they let prisoners fish and keep whatever they catch. It's open air so you wouldn't be cramped into a room like this. If you want, I've an old watch I can bribe a guard with to get you on the list. The first load leaves tomorrow. Many of the men here want to go, but the guards only choose the healthiest, as you have to ride a train to get there. Now if you don't want to go, that's you're business, but if you stay here, you're not likely to live more than four or five months. I'm too old to go and I've been here two months as it is. They won't take me and I've been hoping for a young man such as yourself that I can help. At least I can make my last days useful for something. What do you say?"

I agreed and he emptied his pockets of a tin cup, pencil, writing paper, and a fork. I couldn't believe he was giving me all this, but I couldn't argue with him. He figured he was going to die soon and they'd take it off his body like a pack of buzzards anyway. He'd taken a liking to me, saying I looked like his boy. He didn't know where his son was. They'd both joined up together, Lewis thinking he could keep an eye on him, but they got separated during the Battle of Chickamauga.

I thanked him over and over, but he said, "Don't thank me, John. I can't tell you exactly where you're going or what it's going to be like. I know you'll die if you stay here and I hope you'll at least have a chance somewhere else. Good luck."

After a few days, I was chosen to go on the train that was leaving March 12th. All of the men who were chosen were happy, talking about how great it was going to be at this new camp where we'd be able to live outdoors. I said goodbye to Lewis and boarded the train. As we climbed into the cars we kept looking around for another train to pull up, but it never did. We couldn't figure how we were all going to fit. The guards lowered their guns and kept telling us to load and push back. By the time the doors were closed, the car was silent. We were standing looking at each other without room to sit or move. The train started and we rode for hours and hours until it turned into days and days. A couple of men were sick and then it made all the men around them sick. We yelled and begged for the train to stop, but it kept rolling. When it did stop for water or coal, they wouldn't let us out. Finally, after what seemed like a week of hell, the train slowed down and the doors opened. We were all so glad to get out of that awful car. I remember the tall pine trees as we were marched a few miles to the prison. When we arrived at the gate, one of the prisoners asked where we were. The guard looked at the man and grinned, "Why you're at Camp Sumter, here in Andersonville, Georgia."

I'm going to wait as long as I can to write again, as I've only got room for one more letter and that'll be it if I don't get out. Remember, you have to go back to the start and turn a quarter turn to the right.

September 21st, 1864

Dear Jimmy,

I know it's been a long time since the last letter. I'm afraid now if I wait any longer I won't be able to write it all down.

I still remember when we looked through the gates of the north entrance. It has two sets of great, wooden doors. As soon as we looked into the prison yard, the man in the front of the line started crying, "No. Oh please God, no. Please let me go back!" We stopped, but the guards kept pushing us forward into the prison. I've been told the whole area is twenty-six acres, but there were about 30,000 men living on it. And the middle of it was a swamp where nobody could stay, so it was really smaller. We saw the stream for fishing. It was a nasty little creek with all sorts of filth, hardly more than a few yards across. On either side was the swamp with great bugs flying around, biting the poor souls. I'd always wondered what the Bible meant when it talked about a wretch. Now I know. Any man who drank the water did so only to be pardoned from this awful life. And there were quite a few who did.

There were no living quarters for us. A man took whatever he had to make a kind of small tent. Any kind of shelter is called a shebang. When we first entered the camp, it was like jumping into an icy pond. We just stood there looking as these animals that used to be men swarmed towards us. Compared to the prisoners here, the men in Richmond were fat and jolly.

As we stood there, there was a large mob asking us all sorts of questions. "Where's Grant? Is he coming for us?

Where's Old Bob? Have they caught him yet? Were you captured trying to rescue us?" Sadly we heard that last question a lot. We of course answered "no" or "I don't know" to just about all of them. But at the time we were just trying to stay on our feet and not kneel down and cry, even though there were a couple of men who did just that. Lewis had told me before I left, "You don't have to be mean, but don't look weak." I did the best I could but at the time I was so disappointed in the camp I really didn't care. I saw the thin, hollow faces of the prisoners but I didn't look at anybody in particular. I heard a voice that sounded like it was addressing me but I ignored it. Then the voice was louder,

"Where'd you get the cross pin, friend?" I didn't look up. I just stared at the ground. It was the lowest I've ever been in my life. I didn't even stutter.

"A friend. Annie."

"This one's mine. John, come with me." I woke up and there was Sam Flint. He'd lost at least 75 pounds and was filthy like all of the men. I would have never recognized him but he recognized the cross and then me. He came and put his arm around me and walked me back to his area. He seemed kind of pushy to get me away from everybody else and was looking around a lot, making me nervous. When we finally got to his living quarters, he explained that all the new prisoners, or fresh fish, were being scouted out by the clans. These clans were groups of men who would act friendly to a man when he first arrived and then that night they'd come and take whatever he had. Sometimes they'd beat him up. Other times they'd kill him. There'd been no punishments so far for the crimes. The officer in charge of the camp was a grouchy foreign captain who didn't care how many of us lived or died so long as we stayed within the walls. Sam said I could stay with him and the other boys from Kentucky, but I'd have to ante in something valuable, especially gold.

At first I showed him my cup, but he quickly pushed it back to me, saying, "No. You can't live without that. You need to put in Annie's pin." I started to speak. I'd rather cut off my left arm than give up that pin.

"You'll get it back, I promise. We guard these with our lives." I slowly took the pin off. I kept looking at it but didn't say anything. He was quiet and stood there staring at me.

"We've all had to give something that's important to us. That's what being a part of this family is about. Everyone sacrifices but that means we stand up for each other when the time comes. Once you put that pin in the bag then there's a dozen men who'll kill anybody who tries to hurt you. Besides, we've heard Grant is coming through here any day now."

If it weren't life or death I wouldn't have parted with it, but since I chose life over death for her, I didn't think she'd mind. Besides, what choice did I have? I finally said okay and he disappeared for a minute and then came back with a black pouch. He opened it up and I dropped the pin down and heard it clink on other metal. He quickly closed the pouch and went back behind a curtain where a couple of men were standing. I hadn't noticed before, but now I saw they were guards for that little pouch. On the one hand those men were willing to kill for what may have been worth five dollars, but on the other hand, that pouch held the most precious items that any of us had. When Sam came back he introduced me to the other men. Some gave firm handshakes, one even hugged me. I had no idea at the time how close we would become. If I had more paper I could write for days about all of my new friends, but there just isn't the space.

Sam told me all about different attempts to escape too. There were two walls in the camp. The outer wall, which was made of tall pine trees tied together and an inner wall which was much shorter. The inner wall was called the dead line, cause if you crossed it you were dead. There were no questions, no excuses, no second chances. The guards sat up in little boxes at the corners, called pigeon roosts. Their guns were loaded and they didn't mind knocking off a prisoner every once in a while just to fight boredom. Those who did escape usually didn't get too far. A few local farmers were paid to catch any escaped prisoner and they had dogs trained to track men. Even if a man escaped, he was so weak he couldn't run fast. Besides, he's deep in Georgia. If anybody saw him he'd get captured or shot. I never tried to escape but I don't blame the men that did. They would rather die as a man than live as a rat.

I didn't know it at the time, but the gifts Lewis gave me were the most valuable possessions I ever owned. Those few items kept me alive for many months. I'm considered a salty fish now as I'm a prison veteran. Of course Sam was right about the tin cup. Without a cup to catch water, men die within a week, sometimes less if it's hot. Without a pencil and paper, men lose hope and die within a few months. After I'd been here a couple of months, I lost hope too. Especially seeing how the clans of robbers beat and killed their own kind, just for a knife or watch. Then one day, the Confederate camp commander, Captain Wirz, finally had enough complaints and allowed a court of prisoners to bring the chiefs of each clan to justice. There were six chiefs and they were all hung. One of them was hung and his rope broke, so he was hung again. I wish it'd happened to all of them. With the raiders gone, groups were formed and men worked together to help keep more of us alive.

I'm sure it's been hot up there in Kentucky, but you have no idea of the heat in Georgia during July and August. After the first week in August, men were dying fast from thirst and then diarrhea. The thirst was so miserable men would drink from the stream just to make it stop. Everyone was hopeless. We all felt God had forgotten us and we were in hell. We had prayed and prayed without any help. We begged for a sign. If I hadn't had this letter to write, I would've drank from the stream myself. But then at the beginning of the second week of August it started raining and it poured for four days straight. A hard rain, drenching our bodies and washing the camp.

On the 13th, a dark cloud came over the camp. It was so large and black it was unlike anything anybody had ever seen. We were all scared and so were the rebels. Then, out of the cloud came a great bolt of lightning right at a tree stump inside the walls. The stump exploded and water gushed out of it. The water flowed and flowed. And we've had fresh water to drink every day since. We've named it Providence Spring. It's hard to describe how much that spring means to me and most of the men here. I could never have imagined a more God-forsaken place. After being here for eight months with the stench, disease, and death I had lost hope that God even knew I was here. But then the lightning struck and I know He knows. That spring means hope. Maybe one day after the war is over you can come and visit it, knowing how much it meant to me.

Which brings me to today. The rebels are moving some out of the camp. I think our men are closing in and they don't want us to be freed. This time I won't make the trip. I'm too weak to travel. I don't have any flesh to speak of. I'm just a ghost of what I used to look like. I've seen many men that looked like me get sick and none of them lasted long. I started having stomach pains yesterday, which means my time is just about up. I know this is where I'm going to die. I'm going to give my tin cup and fork as well as everything else I have to a boy here so that he'll deliver this letter and the cross or at least give them to someone who will. I hope they make it.

I miss the farm and seeing you and the folks. I miss having a big breakfast with eggs, biscuits, and gravy. I miss not getting to marry Annie and have a family. I miss the children I'll never have.

I'm giving this letter to the youngest man in our group, Jeff Ford is his name. Whether it's him or someone else that delivers it, please be kind and welcome him. Tell all that I love them and that their son and brother died believing that his country was worth dying for.

One more thing, please go back to Annie and let her read this letter. I didn't have enough paper for both of you.

My sweet Annie,

I endured eight months of hell on the chance that I might see you again. I've thought about my choice a thousand times and I don't have any regrets. For that chance I'd endure this hell for another eight months if my body could survive.

Here's my last poem. I hope you like it.

> If my eyes could see one last glimpse, it would be your face.
> If my ears could hear one last sound, it would be your voice.
> If my skin could feel one last touch, it would be your hand.

Take care,
    John

CASUALTY SHEET.

Name: _J. J. C. Gore_

Rank: _Private_   Company: _a_   Regiment: _3_

Arm: _____   State: _Kentucky_

Nature of Casualty: _Death_

CAUSE OF CASUALTY—(Name of Disease, &c.)	BY WHOM DISCHARGED.
DEGREE OF DISABILITY.	FROM WHAT SOURCE THIS INFORMATION WAS OBTAINED.
	Roll furnished by Comy
	Genl of Prisons
BY WHOM CERTIFIED.	REMARKS.
Bvt Maj W. T. Hartz	
_a. a. G_	
DATE OF DISCHARGE, DEATH, &c.	
September 28th 1864	
PLACE OF DISCHARGE, DEATH, &c.	
Andersonville Ga	

Geo W. Sweasting
Clerk.
(149)

Seated: James Marion Gore (Jimmy) holding
Lenwood Gore, Edward Howell Gore. Standing:
James Napoleon Gore (1924)

Andersonville Prison Cemetery

Author's Note

While based on historical events, this is a work of
fiction. Some of the characters are completely fabricated
and any likeness to actual individuals is coincidental.